The Lost Soul
of the Joukhoorei

AF215276

RASHMI NARZARY

Om Books International

First published in 2025 by

Om Books International

Corporate & Editorial Office
A-12, Sector 64, Noida 201 301
Uttar Pradesh, India
Phone: +91 120 477 4100
Email: editorial@ombooks.com
Website: www.ombooksinternational.com

Sales Office
107, Ansari Road, Darya Ganj,
New Delhi 110 002, India
Phone: +91 11 4000 9000
Email: sales@ombooks.com
Website: www.ombooks.com

ISBN: 978-93-6395-803-6

Printed in India

10 9 8 7 6 5 4 3 2 1

Rashmi Narzary is a dog lover at heart, an author by passion and an independent editor by profession. Awarded the Sahitya Akademi for Children's Literature in 2016 for her collection of short stories, *His Share of Sky*, creative storytelling and reimagination of folklore and legends are her forte.

Literarily, socially and academically acclaimed, her debut novel, *Bloodstone: Legend of the Last Engraving*, is one such fiction woven around the chronicles and legends of the famed Kamakhya Temple of Assam. Her second novel, *An Unfinished Search*, is a historical fiction set in the Indo-Bangladesh border at Karimganj, portraying the rootlessness and loss of identity that war and partition of nations cause. Her seventh book, *Whistles of the Siphoong: Tales from Assam's Bodo Heartland*, is a moving, lyrical narrative of stories inspired by lore, legend, culture and life of the Bodos of Assam, told through the mesmerizing music of the flute. *The Lost Soul of the Joukhoorei* is her eighth book.

She received the Prag Prerona Award for Literature, 2020. Narzary's work is being taught in universities and researched for doctoral thesis and has been translated into other Indian and foreign languages.

Her growing-up years in Shillong, where she started her education in Pine Mount School, left an indelible, endearing mark in her bond with the hills and nature. Little wonder then that an abundance of nature rules her otherwise simple, easy narrative style. Her driving passion for storytelling made her degree in economics and post-graduation in Human Resource Management take a backseat.

She lives in Guwahati with her husband, a former IAS officer, in a home that abounds with pets and large flocks of visiting birds.

JOUKHOOREI
/jō/kho͞o/rā/
noun

Derived from the Bodo words *jou*, meaning wine,
and *khoorei*, meaning bowl.

The joukhoorei is the dry shell of a gourd with
its insides scooped out to hold liquid. In
Fhuwanji, it is mostly used to hold jou, or wine.

To Ronie,

Now past the snow on Mount Swrang
Into infinity and beyond
Yet with us, in the songs you've sung
And the love you've left behind.

Contents

Why It Happened

Prologue

To Creation,
There never was a beginning
Nor will there ever be an end.

But in the time and space in between, there are often surreal occurrences, which lie beyond the realms of understanding, to baffle all human reasoning. There have been mystical connects that surpassed all barriers of rationale and worked their way through different time spans in Creation. Through different space and incarnations, these gave rise to events that people in the village of Fhuwanji and in the Umata farm higher in the valley of Kindoree felt were paranormal. Yet others felt these were normal, but not before they had been drawn into that string of random events that gave birth to *The Lost Soul of the Joukhoorei*. All these people also found that each was playing a significant role in this supernatural drama of Creation, without really realizing it.

However, what seemed to be random occurrences to the simple, contented people of Fhuwanji and Kindoree, and of the Umata farm, were actually predestined. For, in the Universe, there is nothing random, there is nothing coincidental. Everything is preordained.

As said Old Monk, 'That which is destined to be, will yet be…'

Like the joukhoorei. Now, the joukhoorei was an inert and humble part of Creation and yet, it was thus predestined that from it would unfold the amazing journey of the lost soul, the hundredth Jerutu. During that journey, it would put many through test, grief, joy and then lead into ultimate salvation. The joukhoorei itself was a bulb-shaped bottle gourd, with its flesh scooped out and the shell dried, to be used as a container, wherein a kind of rice beer called jou is stored.

This is a tale of having and losing, of uprooting and settling, of the joys of befriending and the pains of then letting go, of finding and surrendering and of fighting an inner battle of moral dilemmas, of the interests of the self, pitched against the greater interests of the ultimate truth of the Cosmos, of mortal attachments and immortal detachment, of Maya and Nirvana. It is a tale of a soul not lost forever but a soul who had only lost its way.

So said Bathou. So said Shiva.

It is a tale that will be told over and over, to echo far beyond the Dorai range and the Himalayan foothills to reach out to people all over.

So said Bathou. So said Shiva.

Where It Happened

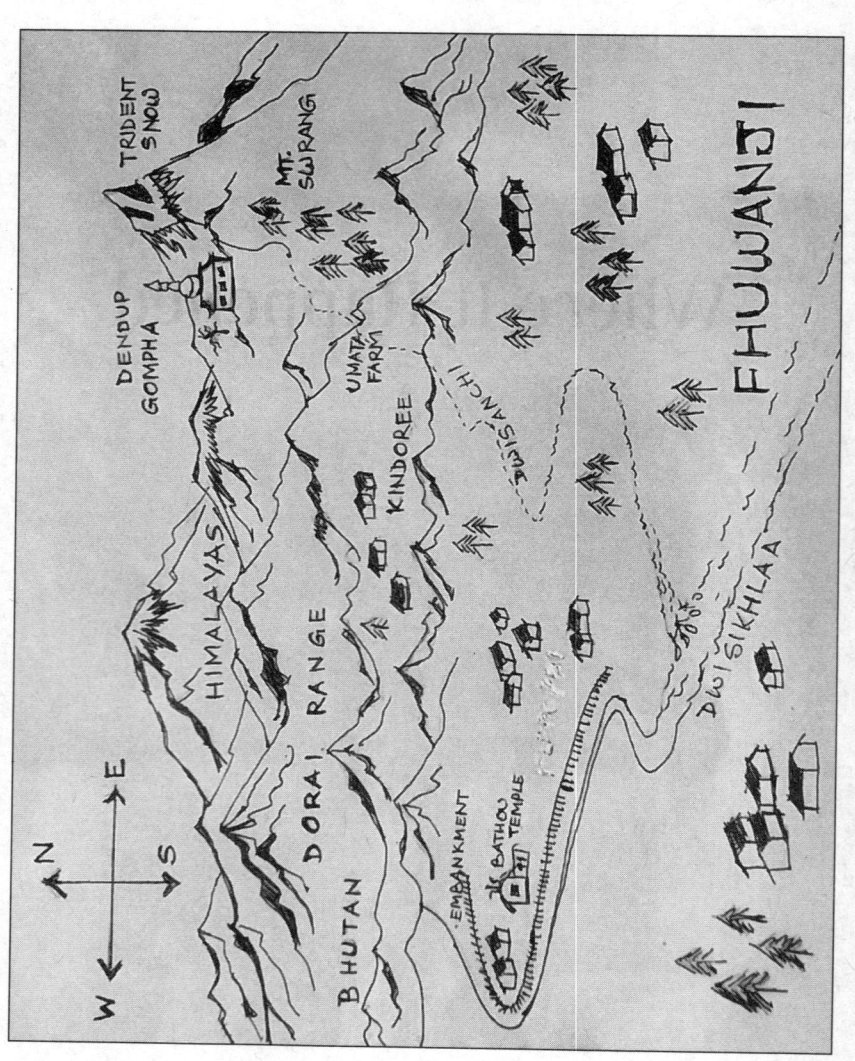

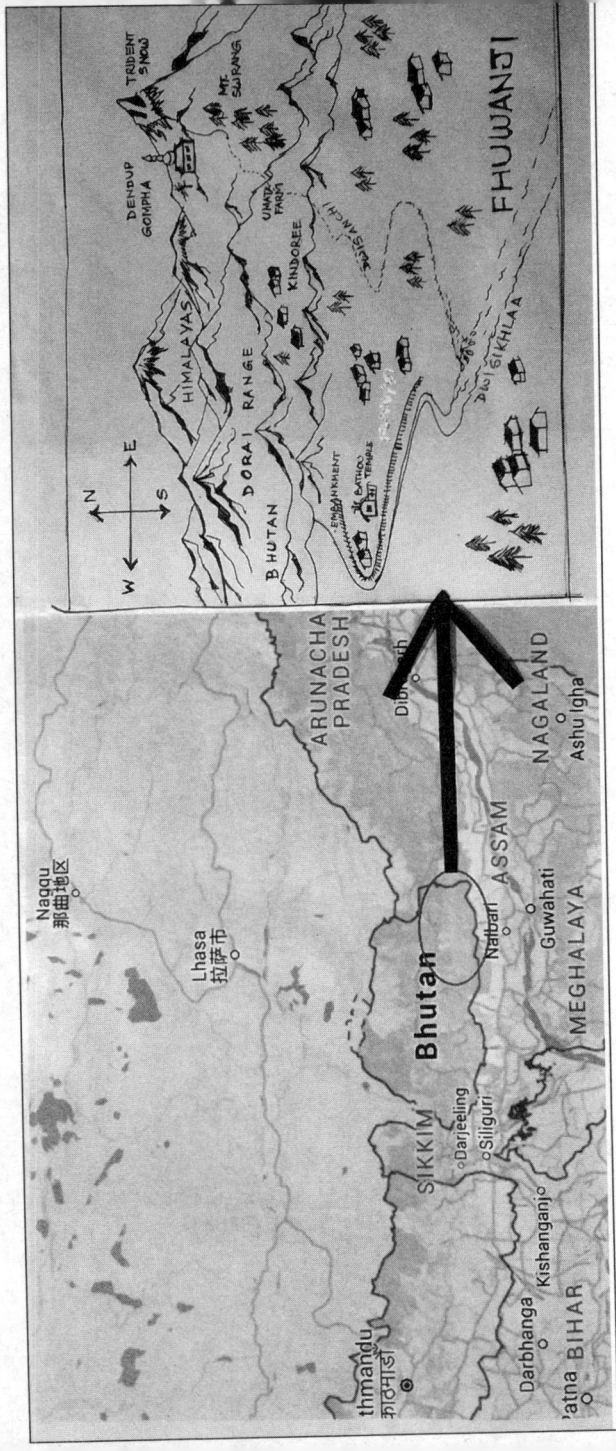

How It Happened

1

Baulungbwrai

Old Baulungbwrai never wakes up.

And on those rare occasions when he did, he instinctively reached for the aged and browned dry gourd shell that hung from a length of jute rope, looped around his neck like a garland. Wilted by wind and moistened by sweat, the rope had been rubbed smooth against his skin over time. The dry gourd shell with its small mouth, narrow neck and large round belly, hung like a pendant from the rope garland. Every time old Baulungbwrai came out of his stupor, he reached for his gourd shell, brought it to his drooping lips and poured from it a generous gulp of the smoky liquid down his throat. Ah! How sweetly pungent the drink was, almost divine! It carried the old man to a state of being blissfully floating in Heaven.

Feeling no pain, no sorrow,
Wishing for no gain, no morrow.

Little wonder then that Baulungbwrai never wished to come out of the stupor of that divinely acerbic drink. That rice beer. Jou, he called it. And he took it to his lips.

Then on, his narrow slits of eyes remained open for a while as if to take in enough air for the next long plunge into oblivion. And before he even realized, he had already taken the plunge. Baulungbwrai was asleep again.

Baulungbwrai never wasn't.

The oldest among the old in the village of Fhuwanji, in the foothills of the Himalayas near Bhutan, didn't remember ever seeing Baulungbwrai young. As far back as time and the mind would go, Baulungbwrai was always known to be old. Very old. And always sitting or lying about the Bathou temple in the village of Fhuwanji, on the banks of the Dwisikhlaa River that flowed all the way down from some snow mass in the high Himalayas. He was almost a relic, an inseparable part of that century-old Bathou temple.

The temple too was as unassuming as Baulungbwrai himself. It was made of just a tin roof supported on four crooked tree trunks. Sheltered on the ground beneath this simple structure was the erect stone structure, symbolizing Lord Shiva. A low wall of about a foot-and-a-half from the ground, made of reed and mud, ran along three sides of this shelter, leaving the west open. A longish shed of bamboo and thatch, supported on trunks of the betel-nut tree, extended outward from this open side of the altar. This was meant to provide shelter from rain and sun as devotees offered prayers to the stone structure which they believed to be their god Shiva. Bathou.

That stone structure however stood in all its raw magnificence, in contrast to its immensely humble shrine, without ever being fine-shaped or smoothened. It thus retained every element of creation's mystic and awe for the religious soul. Rising from an oblong stone base, it wouldn't be more than two-and-a-half-foot high and finished off with a rounded top. A queer rise and fall of grooves and patterns marked the stone all over, in what seemed like a very systematic haphazardness. The temple's floor was of silt, like the kind that settled along river banks and made up the soil of riverside villages.

Whoever visited the Bathou temple, did so partly to pay obeisance to the stone image of Shiva but mostly to see the old man, Baulungbwrai. And no one ever missed him. He was always there with his gourd shell hanging around his neck. At his most upright, which was a rare occasion though, the topmost part of Baulungbwrai's head must have reached not higher than five feet and a couple of inches from the ground. A piece of cloth indulgently draped itself round his belly above the naval and reached down to the calves on his stocky legs. As for the upper part, no one ever saw what he wore there. The reason being, over and above every inner garment, a loose robe of some thick fabric always hung upon his body. When it was new, this robe probably restricted the movement of Baulungbwrai's legs. One was led to suppose this because the robe had a long, vertical tear on one side from the thigh down, made by forcing the cloth apart by hand. Neither could anyone tell what the colour of that fabric ever was when it first arrived upon Baulungbwrai's plump body. A thick length of rope wound itself twice round his waist over the robe before the ends got tied together by another smaller and thinner bit of rope. A hood was attached to the robe and Baulungbwrai always had this hood covering more than half of his face. Because during the day, sunlight bothered him all the while as he lay in his slumber and during the night, it was the chill wind from which he covered his face. So very few got to see the face behind that hood.

A number of cloth pouches, their sizes ranging from that of a small onion to that of a large guava, hung from the rope around his waist. Because he carried all his earthly belongings on his earthly person. People imagined those pouches to have coins or beads or even dried plums and roasted rice flour. But then it was just that, people's imagination. For no one got to see what those pouches really had inside them. Baulungbwrai also wore strings of beads around his neck over the hood and around the wrists. Some of these beads were dull in colour, like rudrakhsh and tulsi. Others were brightly coloured, like those of the Nepalese, and of some tribes in the mountains of Arunachal Pradesh. The few who got a glimpse of the face behind the hood on a rare occasion, said that there was a sparse growth of hair on his round head. There was another growth of sparser hair, so they said, which just about managed to pass off as eyebrows. And on his chin grew a countable number of hair, which ran down for an inch or two before finally giving up. Irrespective of the old and the young, people just seemed to adore Baulungbwrai the way he was, even though they hardly got to speak with him or saw him smiling at them. For he was always in his own world of blissful stupor.

The gourd shell itself was always full. With jou. No one filled it though. It just never got empty. The more Baulungbwrai drank from it, the more seemed to appear from some magic spring inside the gourd shell, thus keeping it always full. The old in Fhuwanji said that decades ago, before breathing his last, the Bodo priest of the Bathou temple mentioned something of a spirit which made its home in gourd shells, though only after much fuss over which gourd shell to make its abode in. Such chosen gourd shells, the priest had said, were called joukhoorei. After the spirit had chosen one such shell as a joukhoorei, he never forsook it. Because though the spirit itself was only air, it drew its sustenance from remaining immersed in fluid, in that divine brew, and made the joukhoorei replenish itself with as much rice beer as and when Baulungbwrai sipped from it. So that when the joukhoorei remained full, the spirit too could happily remain immersed in it.

The spirit of the joukhoorei, however, had the ability to refill it only when someone drank from it regularly. If sipping from the joukhoorei ever stopped for whatever reason, the dying priest had said, the spirit's ability to refill it too would stop. And then the joukhoorei would cease to be refilled on its own. As such, there would be no more rice beer in it. With no rice beer and no fluid, the joukhoorei would become dry and the spirit of the joukhoorei would no longer be able to survive in it. It would then be forced to leave the joukhoorei to go out in search of another such home with fluid in it. But even there, the same tenet would remain; the spirit would be able to refill the vessel only if someone kept drinking out of it.

The priest also mentioned that the spirit in the joukhoorei expressed its gratitude by granting divine bliss upon the one who always kept it replenished and full by unceasingly sipping from it. The priest, however, refrained from mentioning if drunken stupor was that bliss.

Those same old folks also told tales about sightings of a mermaid in the waters of the Dwisikhlaa just near the temple, but only on certain full-moon nights. She had a charming shell upon her back, like that of a turtle. So the old folks began to call her Mertle. She was as legendary as Baulungbwrai but very few saw her. That's why many thought her to be only imaginary. However, as Fhuwanji's fate would have it, those who heard the old Bodo priest's dying words and those who had visions of Mertle, were themselves very old now and so people shrugged their words off as blabber of the senile. And as decade after decade passed by, this legend of the spirit in the joukhoorei too died and got buried in the silts of the Dwisikhlaa. But Baulungbwrai lived on. And sipped on. Old as ever, blissfully drunk as ever.

And the Dwisikhlaa flowed on, beholding all time and event that passed Fhuwanji by.

❧

Then happened the great deluge.

That year Fhuwanji reeled under the worst flood ever since time and the village came to be. Until then, the Dwisikhlaa never once came up to the threshold of the Bathou temple. According to the villagers, that was Dwisikhlaa's way of remaining small before Bathou; that was her way of showing her reverence to her god. But on that catastrophic monsoon night in that fateful year, heavy rains up in the mountains of Bhutan suddenly fed the upper courses of Dwisikhlaa with gushing rainwater, loosening rocks from the mountains and eroding red earth from the valley. The Dwisikhlaa turned invincible that night with the fury of the storm. Foaming, frothing and berserk as she hurtled down the mountains, she forced apart the embankment which so long kept Fhuwanji safe during the rains from the turbulence of the innumerable, serpentine mountain streams that flowed into each other and raced down as one wild river, the Dwisikhlaa.

So, like never before, that year Dwisikhlaa forgot how much she revered Bathou. She forgot that she never came up to his threshold. Because that night, like in a trance of some mysterious power, like a woman possessed, Dwisikhlaa not only swelled till her banks overflowed and inundated Fhuwanji overnight without any alarm, but she also spilled over to reach the Bathou temple. She swept past Bathou's threshold into his altar and with an unimaginable ferocity, started reaching up the sacred stone. While her waters created havoc among the sleeping folks in Fhuwanji, catching them unawares, she herself rolled into tiny brisk waves that feverishly lapped up the stone shivling and lashed down to its base only to rise and fall back again and again with gaining rapidity. And all along, Baulungbwrai lay there in his drunken stupor under the temple's shed. Then just before daybreak, Dwisikhlaa calmed down. She gave one last lap up the stone structure, this time with the gentleness of a wash after the defiling and sank away to the base of the oblong stone platform on which the shivling sat. Elsewhere around Fhuwanji, the waters still surged. The vicious currents that took with them cattle, human, homestead and grain were yet to ebb.

But Dwisikhlaa would go back to revering Bathou as before, never disregarding him, let alone crawl up to his threshold.

That was the last deluge Dwisikhlaa created.

All through that fateful night and through the next morning, villagers in Fhuwanji waded about in shock and panic. Men tried to wrest out from the river downstream whatever life was swept away and women tried to carry to dry, loftier ground whatever food-grains, poultry, clothes and utensils they could save. Old folks cried, cursed and prayed. Petrified children hid inside empty baskets in the granaries or screamed from the top of thatched roofs. Some cried over lost pets, some were bemused over other people's pots and pans floating by their yards and yet some clung to their mothers in absolute terror. And now the menacing clouds, thunder and lightning all moved together from the lower Himalayas towards Fhuwanji.

The night was sinister and dark at Fhuwanji, while the sky above it was overcast. Bisron, Gabkho, Pali and some more youth waded through the muddy, swirling flood waters to the Bathou temple to bring Baulungbwrai to dry ground, though they expected the temple yard to have been saved from the ravage. But when they reached there, they saw that the temple yard too was in knee-deep water. Only the oblong platform, on which the erect stone stood, remained above water. Around the altar, the waters frisked the boys' ankles. But old Baulungbwrai, the very soul of the Bathou temple, was nowhere.

Bisron and Gabkho ran towards the river, desperately hoping to find the old man lying somewhere in his usual comforting, drunken stupor. Pali went hurrying back to the village to inform the elders. A drizzle started. Deafening thunder rolling down from the Himalayas towards Fhuwanji was heard at a distance. Bisron and Gabkho didn't speak a word but all of a sudden, to each came dismal recollections of what the old folks had said, that as long as Baulungbwrai lay slumbered and drunk in total bliss somewhere in the yards of the Bathou temple, Fhuwanji would remain in an equal bliss. But from the hour Baulungbwrai would no more be there,

Fhuwanji's destiny would change. It might then touch great highs or it might then touch great lows but its destiny would change for sure.

Maybe the time for that change had arrived.

Baulungbwrai was now nowhere near the Bathou shrine, nowhere as far as the eyes could see. Soon the village elders arrived at the temple yard, among them old Pholey Deehang and Girim Umata. The drizzle was slowly turning into a downpour. Pholey Deehang and Girim Umata were both greyed of hair and wise of head, farsighted men to whose words the villagers lent all their compliance and respect. There were also pious souls who otherwise worshipped at the shrine every dawn but now came just to see how even the gods could become so wrecked and helpless. If Bathou himself could be so, what should befall the villagers? They moaned and distressed over the fate of the coming days. There were no spoken words but a tacit exchange of feelings. Of doom and despair, of what was to be done next. The air was filled with wails of human and cattle, the intermittent pelting of rain, and a mocking whistle of the cold, moisture-laden wind. Baulungbwrai had not yet been found.

'But Baulungbwrai may not be gone,' someone whispered, encouraging more whispers and fears to be spoken out.

'Will the prophecy come true?'

'What if it does?'

Having remained quiet all along and looking around to take stock of things, Pholey Deehang at last spoke. Despite his advancing age, he was erect of posture and amazingly focused of mind. However, if his wrinkled skin was stretched taut, it would cover his body twice over. Nevertheless, now he spoke.

'Spread out, boys! Go, call more men from the village. Go in search of our old man. Net the river downstream, look into the backwaters. Look into crevices of the eroded bank. Oh God! Find him! We will be, only if he is ... Go now! Move out in every direction you can, boys, go!'

Young boys and men broke out in as organized a manner as they could in that situation of disarray and calamity. Groups moved out with fishing nets, lanterns and sticks in their hands. And immense hope in their hearts.

Bisron meanwhile listlessly walked towards the erect stone, the symbol of god on earth. Long, matted strands of water weed and grass, brought by the flood waters, were left clinging upon the stone organ, though the waters had receded. These creepers now lay partly hanging towards the back of the stone shivling. Bisron walked towards the back of the shivling, all the while hoping someone would shout and call him from a distance to tell him that they had found Baulungbwrai in a blissful stupor on dry ground elsewhere. He also kept thinking of the night's disaster, of where people would relocate, and of the foreboding that if Baulungbwrai was no more, would they too cease to be? Would Fhuwanji ever remain?

Farther down, Dwisikhlaa had started flowing right across the village. She was still hysteric in her pace, swollen and wide, bearing foam, froth, mountain rocks, mud, uprooted trees and carcasses, of both human and animal. And she was devouring yet more, devouring all that came in her way. Gloom and havoc loomed heavy upon Fhuwanji. Dwisikhlaa brimmed over into acres and acres of paddy field as she carved for herself a new course. Pholey Deehang's family moved out of her way, abandoning their hearth with little else other than their lives and their remaining livestock, to higher in the hills. They would wait up there hoping that Dwisikhlaa would recede and retreat someday, so that they could return to their land and rebuild their home.

And back in the yard of the Bathou temple, Bisron's thoughts came to an abrupt pause when he noticed that among the matted strands of weed upon the shivling hung that same loop of jute rope that hung around Baulungbwrai's neck till the previous day. The joukhoorei still hung like a pendant from the rope. Only, it was now around Bathou. As if Baulungbwrai hung it up with the lord himself for its safekeeping. It had no jou but Dwisikhlaa's waters in it. Never before had villagers seen Baulungbwrai and the joukhoorei separated from one another. Bisron's worst fears about Baulungbwrai were confirmed.

Baulungbwrai was no more.

❧

Girim Umata had seen two and sixty monsoons lash by but never, in all those years, had he seen such a curse sweep through Fhuwanji. That one ominous night took away from him what he lovingly raised over all these years; his strong, youthful son Keihoong. He never returned since he had run out into the frenzied Dwisikhlaa to lug out their neighbour's child from being swept away. Devastated and on the verge of insanity, Keihoong's wife Neishri had put her infant daughter in the arms of Girim Umata and pulled away from hands that tried to stop her from running out into the stormy riverside that night. She had run in search of Keihoong. People watched helplessly, some screaming and pleading her to return. But flashes of lightning only showed them glimpses of her petite silhouette dashing towards the river like another hurricane. Even as they watched in horror, she had slipped and fallen into the swollen river. And after one last and desperate cry for help, she got sucked into the rapacious, rushing waters. The winds howled and the waters roared, united in their evil triumph. Those who were standing there that night and watching had said that they saw for a fleeting moment, just as Neishri fell, a mermaid with a turtle's shell appear above the waters. Mertle. And then as if Mertle had appeared only to take Neishri with her, both vanished together into the dark depths of Dwisikhlaa.

The nightmare lasted for three full days and three full nights. Then on, the clouds of doom passed farther south. The rains ceased. But Baulungbwrai was never found. Fhuwanji's destiny moved towards the most wretched of lows, just as the prophecy had foretold. Dwisikhlaa changed her course and eroded away massive chunks of mute, defeated earth from right under homesteads and growing paddy, swallowing much of Fhuwanji. Most of the villagers abandoned their homesteads to seek refuge elsewhere. But there were others too who refused to leave their hearths and roots. They just awaited their turn to be swept away and be buried into the river's depths, holding on to happier memories while still hoping that Baulungbwrai would reappear as suddenly as he had disappeared, to shepherd Dwisikhlaa back to her original canal.

Girim Umata had arrived upon the dusk of his life but the infant that Neishri had left in his arms was in the dawn of hers. For himself, he had nothing left to live. But for the grandchild in his arms, he had everything to look forward to. It pained his more than sixty-year-old heart to let go of the bond with his roots. Yet, the toothless gums that smiled up at him from his arms convinced him that he could still create roots elsewhere for her. Along with her, for himself too. He decided he would go away from Fhuwanji when there was still time, and ground beneath his feet. He would go away to higher in the hills. He would do what he did best; raise a farm, and therein raise Keihoong's and Neishri's child. His grandchild. He would live life all over again.

He cried. She smiled.

He shivered at the loss of his children. She reminded him that they lived on in her.

He felt lost. She placed her tiny palm on his bosom to reassure.

Thus, old and young harboured hope of new life with each other.

They would start life afresh.

Girim Umata paced about his house all of that night, wondering what to take with him and what to leave behind. He knew, whatever he would leave would be swept away. Everything in the house reminded him of Keihoong and Neishri. Outside, he heard his horses neigh. Those, Girim Umata knew, were cries not raised out of hunger but out of a premonition of the approaching catastrophe. He wondered how he would take care of the infant all by himself. But he had to. He would. For he had to leave that doomed place, taking her with him. And leave he had to, at the earliest. Dwisikhlaa was fast advancing towards his yard. She showed mercy to no one, not to the old, not to the infant, nor to the sick and the dying. His heart cried to stay back upon the land and the home where he lived all his life, to remain with them till fate did to them whatever it willed. And yet, Girim Umata owed it to Neishri to save the infant she had placed in his arms with all her trust before she left to look for Keihoong. That very trust now reinforced his faith in himself. He braced himself for the coming days. He had done it years ago for Keihoong, he would do it all over once more for his child.

Early next morning, Girim Umata put most of his belongings into the cart. He then reined in Barhonka and Poohor, his faithful horses, while their foal Botah walked along beside them. Botah was always content as long as she got to be with Girim Umata and her mother Barhonka, oblivious to all the turmoil swirling around her. The villagers gathered at whatever was left of Girim Umata's homestead, with water sloshing all about their feet, to say their goodbyes. No foot-track along the fields and fallow lands were left dry to walk on. Yet, almost everyone in Fhuwanji arrived to see Girim Umata and his little grandchild, for what they assumed could be the last time.

Pholey Deehang's shoulders shook as he wept. But he did not hold Girim Umata back. He did not have the courage to hug him. He had said, there was no time for that. But the truth was that he was scared he would end up asking Girim Umata to stay back if he embraced his childhood friend at this moment of parting. So he stood at a distance, while tears from an otherwise strong and undefeatable heart flowed out through his hazy eyes and down his wrinkled cheeks, as he watched his friend leave. The other elders blessed the infant and the womenfolk put into the cart whatever they thought the child might need, which the old man might have overlooked. There were goodbyes and prayers, and there were embraces. But Pholey Deehang, with a heart that suddenly felt hollow and sank fast, only tapped at his friend's shoulders as he walked past, leading the horses away. Having gone some distance, Girim Umata looked back one last time to take away visions of Fhuwanji in his mind. And he rode the horses away, past what were fields till a couple of days back, past the village community shed where they sat and celebrated festivals and births, past the school where he brought Keihoong to learn his first alphabets and then past the Bathou temple. All through, the horses never got to walk on dry earth. There was water everywhere. It was up to the horses' knees at places and higher at others. So the hooves were always under water. As he passed by, Girim Umata saw that the shivling stood erect as ever, only now it also had Baulungbwrai's joukhoorei hanging upon it. What he didn't see, nor did he ever come to know of, was that just hours after he had left, Dwisikhlaa had lapped up his home.

But Girim Umata only looked ahead to a new dawn at a new place.

Kindoree.

2

Kindoree

Higher on the Dorai hills, towards the northeast of Fhuwanji, Kindoree's gentle undulation rolled over acres and acres of serene, laidback and charming countryside. From the rolling meadows, the mountains folded up like wrinkles on a giant's sheet, sometimes rugged, sometimes slippery, but always with pretty, tiny, wildflowers and the rarest of rare blooming cacti. It perhaps remained thus, charming and undefiled, only because it was tucked away so furtively among the remote mountains. When clouds swam too low, they almost peeped in through the tiny windows of the stone and log cottages which dotted the entire valley. Chimneys in those cottages started to smoke at the crack of dawn each day, bringing the valley alive with a sense of abundance. On sunny days, bunches of corn and chilli were left hanging from the eaves like lanterns.

Twice a week a bus plied out of Kindoree at the break of dawn to the nearest town and returned from there at dusk.

On both the trips, the bus was more stuffed with passengers than a turkey ever was for Thanksgiving. Its sides bulged out and its roof weighed down. In between these two buses a week, if anyone had to make a trip to town on an emergency, he had to ride on a yak's back or drive a cart drawn by either a horse or a pony. Thursdays were market days in the valley. Money did exchange hands in that market, but a greater part of the buying and selling was still done through barter. Every essential thing, from dung-cakes for fuel to woollen caps, yak-milk chewies, tongs to turn roasting meat in sizzling charcoal, and liver-enhancing herbal balls the size of a pea appeared in the market on Thursdays. Again, if the need for anything else arose in between two market days, people just walked down to one another's homes for the exchange. In the evenings, after the jangle of copper and tin bells around the necks of cattle herded home fell silent, the echo of folk songs rose into the mountains.

It was into that valley of Kindoree that Girim Umata had arrived but had nowhere to put up. Now a kind couple in the valley had their long dead father's room, lying unused, in their modest cottage. So, they let Girim Umata, and his grandchild stay there, sparse though it was, till he made his own arrangements. He tied Barhonka, Poohor and Botah just outside his room and lent the service of the horses to the couple whenever they needed. The couple's children started calling him Grandfather, just as did the couple. Soon, everyone else down in the village of Kindoree too began calling him Grandfather. The young, the old and even those older than Girim Umata himself, started calling him Grandfather. He didn't mind a bit. Rather, it only made him feel grateful that they had so easily and happily accepted him and his grandchild into their midst.

Girim Umata then began clearing a patch of land higher on the mountain slopes. Some days he hired a local boy to do the more strenuous labour but most times, he worked there himself. Sometimes he took the child with him in the horse-cart. He now had a kind of arched roof, made of fine shreds of cane, on the cart. So when the baby slept, he wrapped her in cosy woollens and put her down gently inside the cart under that arched roof, while he worked. At other times when she stayed awake, he tied her upon his chest with a shawl and toiled. Her breath upon his bosom gave him the will and hope, to live and work. And work harder. He soon hired men to help him build his own hut with halved trunks of mountain pine. Just two rooms, but they were his own after Fhuwanji. He also suddenly realized one day that in his subconscious, he even started making plans for the future. Of having a farm someday, one bigger than his land at Fhuwanji, with many farm hands keeping the place abuzz. But right then he felt the urgent need for a caring hand with whom he could leave the child at home while he worked outside on the mountain slopes. He felt guilty of letting the scorching mountain sun shine on the child all day and letting the chill air tickle her pink nose, throwing her into fits of sneezing.

So, the next time when he rode his cart down to the village market to buy provision and sell produce from his small farm, Grandfather spoke to the fodder seller, Sheebleniz, about a nanny. 'Um, well, I am looking for a young girl to be with my infant grandchild,' Grandfather told the fodder seller, 'someone young enough to be playful and old enough to be responsible and caring towards the baby.'

Sheebleniz nodded vigorously. It pained him as well to see the baby always pinned onto Girim Umata, through rain and snow, fever and colic. As it happened in tiny and remote villages where everyone knew not just everyone but their chickens and sheep and the number of caps they possessed too, so did all of Kindoree come to hear of the hard-working old man up on the new farm and his little granddaughter. Folks sometimes walked up to meet him and see his grandchild. Some went to genuinely help and ask if he might be requiring anything. Others went out of curiosity. But none came back disliking either grandfather or the child.

The following week Girim Umata drove his horse cart right up to Sheebleniz's shop in the village market for news of a nanny. He looked around with anticipation but saw no teenager around the shop.

'So maybe no-one's willing, eh?' Grandfather asked, crestfallen.

'Not that really,' Sheebleniz said, dragging a bursting sack towards the front of his shop, 'but the girl I had in mind was sent away to her maternal grandparents, so that she may attend high school. However, if you have no qualms, Grandfather, her paternal grandmother is willing to come and stay with you to look after your grandchild. She will receive as wage whatever you give her. It's your helplessness and the little child, my friend, which have stirred her soul.' He plonked the sack against the wall and stood erect, with his hands on his exhausted waist. 'Hazel is old but she is a capable woman and kind too.'

'Hazel?' asked Grandfather.

'Hazel,' repeated Sheebleniz, 'the woman who volunteered to look after your grandchild.'

Girim Umata fell silent. He never thought of the existence of such an option. He had quite forgotten how it felt to have a woman in charge of his household. And yet, he recalled all those times when the baby had a high fever and he didn't know to do much than to panic and put, as he remembered Neishri doing, a wet cloth upon the child's forehead. And when the fever dropped, he had soaked a piece of muslin in a bowl of goat's milk and put a corner of the cloth into the child's mouth. How hungrily she had sucked on it! When her thirst quenched and her hunger satiated, she stopped sucking and slowly fell asleep. But the old man had lain awake all night. Since Fhuwanji, that night was the first time that he let himself cry. He remembered his wife, how she desperately clung on to him when she died giving birth to Keihoong. He remembered Keihoong, still so young and brave when Dwisikhlaa swept him away. He thought of Neishri. She was more of a daughter to him, though at times she had mothered him too. That night, alone and awake with the sick child, on a land he was yet to feel at home in, he longed desperately to be able to someday go back to Fhuwanji to see his land and his home. He cried, for it tormented him to see the child in pain while he remained absolutely helpless to relieve her of it. He cried like the child on his lap, wishing to be among his people at Fhuwanji.

He didn't know that Fhuwanji was no more.

So, standing there in the middle of the market in front of Sheebleniz's shop, Grandfather was in a dilemma. *Should he say yes to Hazel? Or no?* He had untied the baby from his chest and placed her inside the cart before walking up to the shop. Now, just as he looked towards the cart, the baby wailed out loud. And that wail decided for Girim Umata.

'Is she here this morning?' Girim Umata asked.

'No, but I shall ask her to come tomorrow if the agreement is okay with you.'

'I'll be here, thank you.'

Grandfather once again strapped the baby gently but firmly on his chest with a shawl and stepped into the cart, tugging Poohor to pull the cart homewards. He didn't know what to expect, or how to adapt to the changes that were about to arrive in his life. He had survived enough changes already and he hoped this change would be one for good.

The next day when he came down to the village market, Girim Umata saw a robust woman with Sheebleniz. She looked older than himself, because she truly was. She appeared boisterous too as she helped about in the fodder shop. Girim Umata couldn't recollect ever seeing her on his earlier trips to the fodder shop. He stopped Poohor and got off the cart. Seeing him with the baby, the woman came out to help him and stretched her ample arms forward to hold the baby. Like everyone else in Kindoree, she too knew it was Girim Umata, though she had never seen him before. Not until that moment. The old man let her take the child. There was something comforting about the way she held the baby to her bosom.

'So, what's your name, little one?' the woman asked the baby, expecting her grandfather to reply.

'Dunu,' the old man replied.

'Ah! That's close to Dyunhoo. In my native tongue, Dyunhoo means the golden haired,' she said with enthusiasm. She then gently pushed back the warm cap that covered the child's head, to see her hair.

'Dear me! And she sure has golden hair! My Dyunhoo! My Dunu!'

She pulled the cap back as gently once more over the little head and held the child lovingly against her cheek.

'I am Hazel,' she told Dunu, but actually meant her grandfather to hear.

'Oh, er, yes! Hello, Hazel, I am Grandfather.'

Hazel assumed that's what he wanted himself to be addressed as. A monthly salary was settled and neither side was at all fussy over conditions. They all just got together to raise baby Dunu.

Gradually, Hazel took upon herself to care for Grandfather as well. And no sooner, she was looking after the entire housekeeping of the Umata household as well as the farm grounds. They began having visitors too. Shepherds and woodcutters who saw the new cottage would drop in to say hello. One lazy afternoon, Grandfather saw an elderly couple walking up the hill towards the cottage. The woman sometimes bent over with what seemed to be laughter. She was merrily plump, the man stocky. As they drew nearer, Grandfather saw that each was holding a fowl. When the woman bent with laughter, her fowl squawked and threatened to escape.

Grandfather stepped out as they came nearer. 'Howdy, good folks!' he greeted, 'there being no one around here for miles, I assume you have trodden all the way up to meet us, is that so?'

The man nodded and smiled, while the woman once again laughed, this time slapping the man on his arms. 'You see, Grandfather,' she and the man were both definitely older than Girim Umata, 'Nindamo here is very shy. All the way up here, I have been persuading him to be the first to say hello.'

'Ah! You did?' Grandfather instantly liked their company.

'So I did, Grandfather, but with you greeting first, he was spared!'

She laughed again. The more she laughed, the more the fowls squawked, still in the arms of Nindamo and the woman.

'Open your mouth!' she nudged Nindamo.

'Oh! Well, yeah,' Nindamo chuckled like a teenager, 'so Dailene here coached me to tell you, Grandfather, that,' and he blurted out the words like he was made to learn them by heart, 'this cockerel in my arms and his mate that Dailene is carrying, are our humble welcome gifts to you, Grandfather, the hen here, she is laying eggs. Hazel can cook them for your little, baby, sweetheart...' He paused, as if recollecting what the remaining adjectives of endearment were. The cockerel let out a squawk, releasing his flow of words. 'Angelic grandchild. If you let the hen roost, there will be a cheerful clutch of chicklings for her to play with too. Here, Grandfather, welcome to Kindoree!' And he released the breath that he was holding all the while, making the finer feathers on the rooster stand up. He then extended the cockerel towards Grandfather. Dailene extended her hen too.

More visitors arrived the following week. This time, Thoreo, the meat seller, sent three of his little nephews with a pig and her piglets as gifts for Grandfather. The boys took turns in carrying the basket with the piglets, while the mother pig walked alongside. They brought in a small sack of fodder too for the pigs, to last till Grandfather's next trip down to the valley. Soon, rice cakes, smoked ham and sundried cayenne pepper began arriving too.

As time passed, more animals and poultry arrived in the farm. The farm itself too began to yield a greater harvest. Grandfather was no longer able to manage all of this by himself. So, Dailene had sent her aunt's son, Joyan, to help. Then on, one by one, Minkai, Kelman and Thapa too arrived, and got engaged as farmhands. Soon they all became inseparable extensions of the Umata household, watched over by Hazel.

On sunny mornings Hazel would sit outside by the kitchen on a reed mat, stretch out her legs and put Dunu upon her cushy knees. She put the baby first with her belly on her knees. Hazel would then massage the little girl all the way down her spine and across her little back. Then she turned the baby over so that her back was on Hazel's knees. Then she stretched and flexed the limbs and rubbed her little round belly in gentle, circular motions. The baby gurgled with delight. Each movement of Hazel's hands was so reassuring that a smile, almost divine, spread across the child's chubby face. And all the while, Hazel kept talking to Dunu or singing to her. When she sang, her songs were invariably her own folk songs, sung with a rusty, deep, rising and falling tone, the way villagers in the valley below sang, but in a manner that warmed the cockles of the heart and rang for long in the ears. And so she sang now to the baby on her knees.

> *When the Snow Nymph falls asleep*
> *And winter steps off Kindoree,*
> *When spring arrives with a green sweep*
> *O Mountain Gnome, spin then for me,*
> *Silken yarns of golden sunshine*
> *And of dewy rainbow sparkle*
> *So I may stitch a gown so fine*
> *With my finger in a thimble.*
> *By summer when the gown is done,*
> *On a cloud, to the Snow Nymph let it fly*
> *Past meadows, across the sun,*

And pin it with stars from autumn's night sky.
Then clanging their bells when the sheep come home
They'll rouse the Snow Nymph, make her sit.
Gift her the gown then, O Mountain Gnome
Tell her, the seasons and I made it.
Seeing the gown lying beside her
She'll swirl and dance in boundless glee
Shaking soft snowflakes all over
Ushering winter once more upon Kindoree

Girim Umata's house once more began to come alive. It was beginning to feel like a home.

Then, after a bath and a feed when the child slept, Hazel sometimes took out time from other chores to make pretty frocks with frills and collars for Dunu. If she could squeeze out yet some more time, she embroidered butterflies, rabbits and petunias on the collars. By autumn, she started knitting mittens, sweaters and socks for Dunu. Hazel herself always wore long skirts over equally long petticoats, with a lot of gather at the waist. This augmented her already plentiful middle. Also, Hazel never left her head bare. She always tied a large kerchief covering her hair. So, leaving aside the obstinate strands near the ears, the rest of her hair was always deprived of the beautiful mountain sun. Because Hazel dreaded hair in food, she was scared that an uncovered head in the kitchen would create doom.

But it was her aprons that really stole the sartorial show. They were often longer than her skirts and were almost a shop on the move. Because each apron had many pockets, all in varying sizes, some with buttons and some with horizontal flaps that fell over the mouth of the pocket to cover the opening. These pockets were stitched onto every possible space on the apron. And in them she had an amazing range of titbits, sometimes left there with the assumption that they might be required on the move, and sometimes left there and, well, simply forgotten. But during emergencies, the pockets never failed Hazel. They always produced something that came of help, though not always in the conventional way one thinks of help. Nevertheless, they helped to save the moment. And that was all that mattered during emergencies.

Like the time when an emergency of immense proportions erupted, when the stitches that held the left and right behinds of Thapa's greased and muddied work trousers split in order to accommodate the expanding butts, as he bent to pick a heavy piece of wood. Hazel, who was standing nearby, heard the stitches give way and immediately shut her eyes, fumbled into her many pockets and fished out two thin hairclips, one yellow and the other bright green. Then she gave one brisk look at the parted fabric to gauge the length and location of the split before shutting her eyes again. Then, with deft movements of her fingers, she brought the separated sides together and held them thus while pushing in the hairclips with the other hand, first the green and then the yellow, to finally but momentarily hold the behinds of Thapa's trousers together, until a more permanent solution to the emergency was adopted. And all the while Thapa stood like a statue, scared even to breathe. Thereby, the emergency was dealt with in an unconventional way with whatever came out of Hazel's resourceful pockets. And then Hazel would sigh in relief and whisper to herself, 'Bless the soul who came up with the idea of pockets!'

Hazel made a home out of a house.

On another of Grandfather's trips to the Kindoree valley on a market day, a tiny, brown, unkempt but healthy puppy kept following him wherever he went. When it was time for Grandfather to return home and he climbed into his cart, the puppy sat on his hinds by the cartwheel and kept looking at Grandfather with such doleful eyes that the old man could not help but pick the dog and put it next to himself in the cart. And Brum came home to the Umata farm. But because Dunu could not say brown dog, she would say Brum dog. So the name Brum stuck. Brum didn't much belong to any royal clan but seemed to be steeped in oodles and oodles of loyalty and stupidity at the same time.

Soon winter set in and the snow came.

As many such snows came and went, Dunu too grew up, playing and cuddling with Brum, who began to rule everyone's hearts in the Umata farm. Grandfather had at last begun to see reason to live life once more.

3

The Oowii Oowiis

Dunu had now turned all of ten. She was born with Neishri's soft pale skin but the mountain sun and the carefree runs up and down the valley had caused a healthy tan that brought her pale skin alive. Her eyes were those of Keihoong's. Her father's. Deep and fluid, whoever looked into those brown eyes were magically drawn towards them. And her golden hair ran straight down her nape without any curls or waves, till they reached a little below her shoulders. Hazel would sometimes tie them into two braids and sometimes into one ponytail high on the centre of the head. But most of the time, it was just left loose. In moments such as those, Hazel felt grateful for the ears. 'Praise the kind Lord, my child,' she said, 'for placing the ears where he did upon the human head, as barricades to hair that keep falling forward all over the face!'

Wherever on the farm Dunu stood, she could see the sky bowing down to touch the earth upon the Umata farm far away and all around her, like a gigantic, overturned soup bowl with her little self inside it. The farm rolled out under this bowl, along the slopes of the Dorai hills bordering Bhutan, at the foothills of the Himalayas. On the highest point of the farm stood a pair of tall and graceful coconut palms, the only ones in the whole of the Dorai range. Girim Umata often stood under these palms and gazed for long moments towards the southwest, towards Fhuwanji.

Was it still there? How much of it, if at all? How must Pholey Deehang be? And, above all … might old Baulungbwrai be back? These thoughts often came to Girim Umata and it was as if he shared his past only with these two palms. He let thoughts of Fhuwanji come to him only when he was there with the palms. And before leaving the spot, he cleared out all of Fhuwanji from his being. It slowly became a habit for Grandfather to pat the palms when he reached there, and as he left. A bond began to grow between him and the palms, like a link with the past. He felt as if the palms would someday take him to Fhuwanji. Or bring him news from there or reconnect him to his roots.

However, Grandfather wasn't aware that folks of the neighbouring villages now talked of a serpent, which they believed lay deep within the womb of Dwisikhlaa. They believed the serpent to be Dwisikhlaa's child Jeebou, the one she begot on the night of the deluge by her union with the stone shivling that embodied Shiva. People said that Jeebou now lay under a curse of all those souls who were compelled to leave their mortal bodies, despite a passionate yearning to live. So they had cursed Jeebou, whom Dwisikhlaa brought to life by taking away the lives of so many others. She had devastated an entire generation, in an entire village. Hence, all those souls with a fervent desire to live, but whose lives were wrung out of them, cursed Jeebou...

Forever shall you remain in agonizing hunger and in bodily trauma, as of the very old and the dying! Forever shall you wish to die so as to be liberated from such agony! Yet, death shall not come upon you. You shall live on with your desire to die your death, just as we died with our desire to live our lives...'

The belief went that unable to live such a wretched life, Jeebou did severe penance to Shiva. He hoped to bring to Shiva's realization that, after all, he was one of those same favoured creatures which had the privilege of adorning the matted locks on his head.

'Aren't we of the same ancestors? Then why the favouritism? Why is it that some are allowed to nestle on your hair while I am shoved into the dark underwaters?' Jeebou pleaded before Shiva. 'Let me live my life or let me die my death, Father, I beg you, don't keep me living my death. What fault was it of mine that my mother took all those lives? Why have I also been put to fault for rendering all those children orphans and all those parents childless? Why, Father, shouldn't the curse of the souls be upon the one who caused the catastrophe, and not upon the one who is but a consequence of it? I am that consequence, Father, what fault is that of mine?' Jeebou vowed to continue his penance till Shiva relented.

Shiva, the belief went, slowly opened his eyes. Then he opened his third eye between his brows, which looked like a closed Datura flower in the moonlight.

'Go then, Jeebou, perform me three tasks,' Shiva had said, putting up conditions, 'for each task done, I shall wipe a fourth of the curse and once again close one eye.'

'Father, yet then at the end of the test, won't I be left with a fourth of the curse?'

'Yes, a fourth of the curse shall yet remain and it shall cause you pain. That pain is meant to remain for a reason; it being that your pain shall cause pain to Dwisikhlaa. As you repent, Jeebou, so does your mother. And that shall ease the agony of the souls. But mind you, I say only ease; not wipe away wholly. So shall your curse be eased, Jeebou, but not wiped away wholly!' Shiva told Jeebou.

'And what are the tasks?'

'Fate will take you to certain beings of the Jataka from the ancient past, but reborn in these times to retrieve the lost soul of the joukhoorei. The lost soul being pure and sacred, it cannot be touched by the selfish at heart. But the beings of the Jataka, the ones that I mention, showed selfishness during a past life and for which they continue to spin in the cycle of rebirth, awaiting deliverance. So, in this lifetime, you, Jeebou, shall put them to test. If they fail, they will remain unworthy of bringing back the lost soul of the joukhoorei. And if unharnessed within that phase of the moon when it ought to be brought back, the soul of the joukhoorei will be lost forever. But if they pass the test and prove their worth, their repentance shall be complete and they shall become worthy of rescuing the lost soul of the joukhoorei.'

Jeebou lay his head on the ground and listened quietly while Shiva narrated.

'Your second task will be to bring me a white Datura flower and leave it upon my stone shivling.'

'No other flower but the white Datura?'

'No! No other flower! Did you not know, Jeebou, that the smell of the Datura arouses passion? By leaving the

Datura and its fragrance with me, you shall be leaving all of Dwisikhlaa's passion at my disposal. She shall then no more flow berserk and create no more deluge and destruction. Her energy will then be in my command!'

Jeebou slithered only so slightly as to show that he understood, and that he would obey.

'Lastly, after doing so, slide back into your mother's womb, Jeebou, and remain there for all time to come.'

'Father! But why!' Jeebou twisted.

'Ah! You have not been told, Jeebou, of the Kundalini serpent. She is another of your exalting ancestors. When the slumbering Kundalini stirs, she awakens unthinkably immense proportions of energy inside whomever she stirs. And you, Jeebou, have inherited this virtue of hers. As such, if you stir and come up without my asking you to do so, you shall, like the Kundalini serpent, stir awake Dwisikhlaa's senses. She shall then smell deeply from the Datura. As a result, passion and fury shall reawaken in her. If this happens, Dwisikhlaa shall create merciless deluge all over again.'

Jeebou raised his head from the ground.

'It is for this reason that you shall remain coiled in your mother's womb.'

Dismayed, Jeebou untwisted himself into his full length and lay his head back on the ground.

'As for the one-fourth curse I live with?'

'Ah yes!' Shiva said, 'as for that remaining one-fourth curse, though you shall not remain in hunger and physical pain of the old and the dying, you shall yet live in abstinence like the old. And shall always remain under water, like those dead in the deluge.'

Girim Umata hadn't heard the story of the curse upon Jeebou. Nor did he know that Fhuwanji was no more. He only stood by the palms and hoped that they would take him there someday. Or, that they would bring him news of Fhuwanji.

Ah! Hope…

A few yards away from the palms stood an old oak tree with a hollow halfway up its trunk. A restless mountain stream gurgled across the farm past this oak. Brum always tried to count the ducks there but never could, because they kept moving and confusing him. Tall poplars and firs, large patches of vegetables, corn, stables for the horses and the busy farm hands brought this side of the mountain slope alive. Occasionally, the boys in the farm also saw an owl. He was noticeably big, so they told Hazel, and had white wings that remained overlapped upon his brown chest like a cloak. Joyan, Minkai and Thapa mostly saw him sitting at the mouth of the hollow in the big oak. The oak itself stood at the beginning of a row of fir trees beyond which, in yet another neat row higher up the slope, stood the quarters for the farmhands.

Somewhere along these ten years, Grandfather's small makeshift log cabin of two rooms made way for a comfortable, almost handsome, double-storeyed farmhouse. It had a masculine yet gentle charm about it, maybe because that was the way Grandfather made it to be. Just like him. And like the old log cabin, the new farmhouse too had walls of broad planks of pine. The high roof gently extended down sideways from the centre to form awnings over the many verandas which opened out of the bedrooms.

And with Dunu's bedroom, Grandfather built a special bathroom. He let a handsome ceramic pot that had a lid of some strange tough but even, thin and light substance that was easy to lift and drop, sit on the bathroom floor, for Dunu to sit on and do there what Brum did on the choicest patch of grass outside. Girim Umata also fixed a big, long iron tub in her bathroom. Joyan and Grandfather then painted the insides of the tub a lovely light bluish green, to make it look like the bed of the sea. At the bottom and along the insides of the tub, they painted bright, colourful fish, oysters and pretty shells and seaweeds. So when Dunu splashed the water to make tiny waves inside the tub, the fish appeared to swim ever so gently.

The day Grandfather bought the pot and the tub in the market in town, he sat those in the horse cart with Thapa cuddling the pot like he would a child for fear of the object toppling and breaking. That was a memorable day for the whole of Kindoree. A curious crowd of all ages followed the cart uphill, volleying Thapa and Grandfather with queries about the pot. A few responses from Thapa made some people in the crowd lose their balance with laughter and roll down the slopes, while other responses made them wonder at this amazing pot. Those who rolled down with laughter, never again caught up with the horses pulling the cart uphill, and so they stayed back laughing. Dailene and Nindamo were among them.

The few who managed to walk right up to the Umata farm helped Thapa bring down the tub and the pot and carry them carefully into the farmhouse. Such was the bond among the people in Kindoree, and such was how they embraced Grandfather into their midst. Their huts and fields might have been far apart but their hearts and prayers were with one another.

After Grandfather fixed the pot in Dunu's bathroom, he placed a raised wooden platform behind the pot and on that platform, he placed a tin bucket with a lid on top and a small handle on the upper left side on the outside of the bucket. Now Grandfather cut a big round hole at the bottom of the bucket and placed a valve made of dried fish skin over it. He had bartered the length of fish skin from a gypsy, on a Thursday market in the valley below, for a lantern that Hazel had woven out of pine spikes and studded with tiny green pinecones. How pretty it looked with a tiny lamp sitting inside it! Grandfather also had to part with a jar of pinesap for the fish skin. This valve he fixed with a wire, which went all the way up along the inside of the bucket and got looped to the inside of the handle. Every morning, and whenever required, one of the farm hands carried in water from the spring outside and poured it into the bucket. So when Dunu reached for the handle with her right hand and pressed it down, the wire tied to it lifted the fish-skin valve and made the water in the bucket gush out into the pot, washing away its contents into a covered pit far out at the end of a covered mud drain. How proud Grandfather felt of himself when he had installed this flushing pot successfully!

Grandfather had the windows built big and these he lined with wide windowsills. When these windows were left open during the summers, it felt like the whole hilly outdoors flowed into the house, bringing with them summer's many smells and birdsongs. It was also during the summers that Hazel planted flowers of bright hues in little earthen pots and placed them on the wide sills of the windows. When she watered the plants with Dunu tottering about her, she taught Dunu the names of each colour that enlivened the petals on the flowers. The same plant had so many colours in it that it delighted both Dunu and Hazel. Hazel dressed the windows in soft linen in pastel shades. When the summer breeze teased them, they danced into the house like the wings of a large butterfly.

Grandfather would often carry Dunu on his shoulders and the two would stand looking far away into the mountains from her veranda. She could then see the Dendup Gompa two peaks away. Hazel had her own bedroom and veranda adjoining Dunu's room. Hazel would, when required, stand on her veranda, fill her lungs with air that heaved up her already bounteous bosom, and give one thundering call to whomever she needed to call at that moment—either Joyan, Minkai, Kelman or Thapa. As it sped, Hazel's voice fell and rose in sync with the undulating grounds over which it moved till it fell on the ears for which it was intended. And then the whole body to which the ears belonged darted back in an equal gusto to report to Hazel.

Grandfather was at the head of the line of command. From there it passed down to Hazel and then to Joyan, in that order. Hazel would let farm hands stand outside the kitchen window, their elbows resting on the ledge, and talk to her as she ladled out soup for Dunu or washed dishes at the sink. This is how she kept abreast of exactly how many hens were roosting, how many pumpkins were ready to be picked and when to ask Joyan to call in the self-taught vet from the valley to deworm the pigs. He did this with some herbal powder which Joyan mixed with the pigs' fodder.

During harvests when extra hands were hired, Grandfather put them under Joyan's supervision. Joyan also had a leaning towards carpentry and he made quite a few pieces of furniture for Hazel, to be used in the kitchen. Tables, chairs, stools, and ladders with no more than four or five steps, for Hazel to step up to reach high shelves. Joyan sawed the planks and made the pieces ready for Thapa to nail them together. And when the furniture was ready, Kelman made a kind of varnish with bee wax and paraffin to polish them. This way, the three also got together to make Dunu little toys out of leftover wood. They once made her a little toy-cart out of two boards resting on four little wheels of iron. The cart had a raised wooden border of about six inches all around it. A strong rope was looped to the front border and this served to pull the cart. Dunu would sit inside the cart and hold firmly onto the plank in front. Minkai would then catch hold of the rope and pull the toy-cart all over the farm, with Brum running beside them with his tongue hanging out to catch the summer breeze.

Brum had made several attempts to fit himself into the cart with Dunu, but being larger than Dunu, his behind would always drop off the cart. Dunu laughed with an absolute and unrestrained joy during those rides when the breeze blew her golden hair away from her face and tickled her nose and ears till they turned red. After the run, big boy Brum would let his tongue drool out all the sweat. In the mornings, Brum always accompanied Dunu to school as she walked across the suspended cable bridge over a deep, narrow mountain creek. Sometimes Joyan and at other times Minkai walked Dunu to school. Yet, Brum unfailingly walked beside her for he felt that someone more responsible had to go with them. And when they reached the middle of the hanging bridge, all three used their collective force and swayed from side to side, making the bridge swing and bounce with an equal gaiety. The bridge then felt like it was the mountain fairies' own hammock, hung between two mystifying mountain slopes. They did the same when they returned from school. What fun they had!

It filled Girim Umata's heart to see Dunu growing up amidst such love, laughter and happy abandon. It helped him ease his pains of uprooting. God willing, he would not let Dunu go through what he had undergone, the agony of getting displaced. Grandfather adored the way Brum so possessively watched over Dunu and never left her side. But then Grandpa, as Dunu called him, also loved the way Brum lorded over every chicken, every horse and every sheep in the Umata farm. He roamed the rolling Umata farmlands to sniff out every worm and mole among the vegetables and bark up every tree that had a bird nest hidden among its branches. Sometimes he barked till the annoyed bird eased out white and brown poop upon his big, black and moist muzzle.

And on certain full-moon nights, Brum merely sat on a veranda and gazed at the stream outside that shimmered in the moonlight, cavorting past the farmhouse down the mountain. Grandfather, Dunu and Hazel thought he was just being lazy but only Brum saw what he did. A vision.

Fish? he wondered.

No, human.

Hrrmph! Turtle!

Woof! All three together … oh well! Eventually, Brum was left unsure. And because he got only fleeting glimpses of that vision, he waited patiently in the hope of seeing more of whatever that was.

Then one full-moon night, Grandfather was blissfully stretched out on his rocking chair by the fire inside the house.

Improving times and the mountain air had bestowed upon him a voluptuous girth by now. That happy girth was topped with a pink, bald head with a small circular patch of spiky grey hair floating right at the centre, like a second occurrence of the Arctic Circle.

'This, child,' he was telling Dunu but actually reassuring himself that fate was looking up once more, 'is life. A frothy mug of ale, sizzling slices of bacon straight from the pan with dollops of cheese melting on them, a lovely fire to sit by and warm your palms and wriggle your toes! This is life.'

Dunu giggled without looking up from the matchstick puzzle that she was working on, sitting on the rug beside Grandfather.

All this while, Brum sat looking out of the window, waiting for more of the vision to appear. He didn't know it was Mertle.

Thus engrossed, each in his own bliss, they all missed out on the unique little concert outside, on the mound where the two coconut palms grew. The concert rose by a little fire between the two palms. And the creatures that made merry by the fire, not exactly mysterious lifeforms, were definitely design and experimental embellishments of nature. They perhaps were born to normal farm creatures who knew nothing beyond laying eggs. Or spinning cobwebs in barns. Or being trapped by some farmhand and being roasted for supper. They thought they looked gorgeously different from the rest of their tribe and assumed that they were superior in intellect too. So, they detached from the average farm creature, formed an alliance, and began calling themselves the *oowii-oowiis*. Thus, now it was the oowii-oowiis that were making merry under the alluring full moon up in the skies and a cosily crackling fire upon the ground.

It was around that same time that a gentle whiff of night air fanned the fire by the coconut palms and carried strains of a happy song towards the farmhouse.

Sprinkles of moonshine
Tonight shall cause magic divine
O mortal beings of the immortal earth
Look at the enchanted by birth!

We are not a mys-te-ry
We are no gnomes of fan-ta-sy
We are but the chosen three…!
The oowii-oowii buddies are we
By the barn in the day
We laze around and feed and play
And by the fire on a full moon night
We dance in delight
The oowii-oowiis are we
Yes, we are the chosen three…!

'Hey, listen, Grandpa!' Dunu suddenly sat up and strained her neck towards the window even as Grandpa went on talking to her.

'Do you hear what I hear?' she asked Grandpa.

'Do I hear what you hear?' The old man in return asked himself. 'What do you hear, Dunu?'

'I think it's some kind of a song. Listen…'

'…and by the fire on a full-moon night
We dance in delight…'

Dunu ran over to the window. With one enthusiastic swing of her hand she drew part of the curtain aside to look out towards where the song wafted in from.

'Golly Gimplink! Grandpa! Hazel! Look at that!' and she drew aside the rest of the curtain with a swing of the other hand this time.

'Come, Brum boy! Let's go out and see!' Dunu dashed for the door, with Brum trying to catch the shoes at her feet.

Hazel ran after them.

'Dunu, no! Wait, dear. Let me check out first!'

Hazel looked out of the window and dimly saw the moving creatures by the fire.

'O my Holy Buddha! O dear! What weirdness is all that! Now don't you hurry out like that...' she exclaimed, running after Dunu.

But Dunu had already reached the door and flung it open. Brum dragged his more than hundred pounds of fur, flesh, bones and a collar with a bell, to stand by her. Every now and then he turned back to look at Grandfather and let out a 'gahmurph', beckoning Grandpa to join their little group of bewildered audience. But Grandpa wasn't yet over with wriggling his toes. The rest of them, however, could just about manage to stay without swooning at what they saw.

One of the oowii-oowiis was a fluffed, brown squirrel with a bushy tail, which was by far longer than its agile body and greatly shaggy. As the flames of their little bonfire rose and fell, he stood every now and then on his hind legs and nodded his head towards the other two creatures. Then he wrapped his tail around his neck like a mink fur, and rhythmically bobbed his small head, stretching one fore limb outwards and placing the other on his chest. He was singing his happy heart out. He had a smart orange streak running right down his back from his head, reaching to the farthest hair on the tip of his tail. However, the portion of the orange hair that stood on his head was longer, and grew not backwards like the rest of the orange hair. Rather, they grew outwards from a central point on the scalp. Like the spokes of Dunu's bicycle wheels. The hair reached beyond the perimeters of the squirrel's head and sheltered it like an orange, thatched roof over the brown head.

As the audience in the farmhouse held its breath in sheer bewilderment, they saw that the next oowii-oowii was a handsome rooster. His tail feathers were a brilliant blue, yellow and green and the rest of him was pristinely white. A bright violet, rubbery, goose-bumpy flip of flesh, like the skin of an old toad, rose from his head. From every perceivable angle, that flip of rubbery violet looked like a thickset weathercock of about three inches, balanced upon the rooster's vain head.

And then there was this last oowii-oowii that looked too large and by far less horrifying to be a spider. And yet, it somehow resembled one. Its body was heart shaped, the size of two human fists. It was pink and hairy all over. Its legs were fat around the thighs, fat below the first knee, and fat again below the second knee ... well, fat all over. But between the knees, the legs were short. It was good that its ten legs were fat all over because in any circumstance other than this, the legs would have failed to prop its equally fat body. This thing too was doing the jolly jigs and twirls around the fire. The other two called it Sandie.

Then all of a sudden, the little concert by the fire hastily came to a standstill. The noise of the opening door, the shocked whispers and the sighs of the awed spectators in the

Umata house brought the performers to an abrupt halt. The oowii-oowiis quickly brought themselves to stand in a row, close to one another, and stared back at the farmhouse.

'That's the little girl of the house?' the squirrel gathered his wits and asked in hushed tones.

'Hmm, that she be,' Sandie replied, studying Dunu.

'I just thought her locks were prettier than my tail. Is my tail as long as her locks, by the way?' the squirrel wanted to know.

'Just about so but watch out. There's a dog there. And other humans too, who are bigger in size than the little girl,' observed the rooster.

'So?' the squirrel squinted.

'So?' mimicked the rooster. He always, well almost always, talked better sense than the other two. 'So, our next bonfire is lit farther from here. Or else, we would as well be roasted for supper in that fire inside the house!'

'Me too?' the spider asked.

'A roasted spider for supper? Yuck!' the squirrel teased the spider. 'Yuck again!' and he made mocking noises of throwing up, clutching his belly and bending forward, swaying from side to side.

'Hush, now, hush!' the rooster chastised them.

'Hush!' repeated the squirrel with a paw to his lips, swallowing his laughter and looking at Sandie, 'hush!'

Now the humans in the house and the oowii-oowiis stood facing one another, each in awe and fear of the other and yet too mesmerized to flee. Each waited to see what move the other would make. Sandie had by then slowly crawled up the rooster's neck and perched herself there, in case the occasion to turn around and flee arose. And in the doorway of the farmhouse, a slow but tuneful whistling, as that when wind squeezes itself out from between pressed flesh, floated in and stopped behind the little audience. Grandpa. He had finished wriggling his toes and had now come to join the little group at the doorway.

'Hush, Grandpa!' Dunu said. She wasn't giggling now like she usually did when Grandpa passed wind. Hazel quickly took out a perfumed hanky from one of the many pockets of her apron and held it to her nose. The exercise muffled the words she spoke.

'Nowmph, Gramphfa! That's sure gowfhing to stinkmph like hell wiff all that baconf!'

Grandpa simply ignored all that was being spoken to him and just looked through Hazel as he looked out.

'Now what of that fire there?' his voice boomed through the tranquil night. 'Which farmhand lit it and left it unsanded and unwatered? Does he so want the Umata farm to go up in flames? Hazel? Here, Hazel! Find out which farmhand is being so careless. Early tomorrow morning that unworthy hand ... no ... that whole boy, should be by my wriggling toes!'

'That isn't the doing of any farmhand, Grandpa, look! Look well!' Dunu tried to explain.

'O yeah? Then whose doing is that may I know?'

'Buddha bless our souls, Grandpa, that is the doing of some uncanny beings over there, beings I dare not bring to be by your wriggling toes, not early tomorrow morning, not ever.'

Grandpa at last saw the beings.

'What *are* those things?' Grandpa wondered aloud while the rest wondered silently.

Just as the two opponents stood facing each other, not knowing whether to think of the other as friend or foe, harmless, harmful or plain indifferent, some noise elsewhere broke in through the silence between them. It was a persistent, hacking noise.

Thwak...tho-ee-rk...thwak...tho-kok
Thwak...tho-ee-rk...thwak...tho-kok

As if some supernatural powers had come to solve the confusing situation at Umata farm. Or add to it!

'Isn't the sound coming from the palm fronds, Grandpa?' Dunu asked, looking up at the palm fronds above the concert fire. Hazel was tugging at Dunu with double force now to bring her inside the threshold but couldn't. It only gave rise to a scuffle.

'Sshh!' said Grandpa, looking first at Hazel and then at Dunu. Then he moved his little round eyes towards the palm fronds.

Thwak...tho-ee-rk...thwak...tho-kok

The knocking went on. It seemed to come from some closed object far away. At times it sounded like the pecking of a woodpecker and at other times, like a soft wooden hammer tapping against a tree trunk. Whatever it was, it went on and on, gradually getting louder.

The squirrel hid his body under his mink fur but directed his gaze from under his thatched roof towards the palm fronds. The fronds were still as the night. Yet the noise went on, suddenly changing into something like a large nut rolling down, jumping and bouncing on its way as it came down an uneven trunk of a tree. As humans and animals watched stupefied, a large, green coconut, larger than the normal large, broke free from the base of the palm fronds and slid down the palm tree. It fell to the ground and rolled down Umata farm to stubbornly deposit itself halfway between the two groups of bewitched onlookers. On a sudden impulse, both teams rushed towards the nut, each momentarily forgetting all its apprehensions about the other. On nearing the nut, man and animal all bent down in a circle over the nut to inspect it. The knocking from within went on.

When Dunu found her voice, she poked Hazel's big behind with her small finger and said in an excited whisper, 'Hey Hazel! Look! They're a squirrel, a rooster and a spider alright but aren't they kind of different from other squirrels, roosters and spiders? Exquisite, rather?'

Hazel stepped back and fell in line behind Grandpa, shivering.

A shock-induced 'pwkaak' escaped the rooster when he suddenly realized how close they were standing, unknowingly, to the humans and the big dog. So to disguise his unintended, embarrassing 'pwkaak', he spoke out, trying to make the 'pwkaak' appear intended.

'Hello there! Er, this is me.'

'You are "you"?' Dunu giggled, feeling the tension ease.

'Yeah me…' the rooster stammered.

The squirrel took over the introduction. 'This,' he began, standing on his hind paws and pointing at the rooster, 'is Ronie Rooster. And this,' he said with one fore paw on his own brown chest and smoothening his orange thatched roof with the other, as he bent forward in curtsey, 'is Sunny Squirrel.'

The knocking in the coconut had now ceased. Well, just about.

'Hiyaa bloopity, folksies!' The spider swung down a pink cob string from the rooster's head.

> *Me weave webs in pink*
> *And got them brains to think*
> *Singin' n dancin' n talkin' wonder*
> *Me be Sandie Spider!*
> *And who be you, little miss?*

The knocking in the nut started again. More furiously.

'O yeah! I almost forgot to introduce myself!' Dunu was so perplexed by the strange turn of events this night that she almost thought it was a dream. 'I...'

'Now missy!' Hazel interrupted sharply, 'don't you talk to these beings of the dark!' Hazel tugged at her in panic. 'Turn around, Grandpa, don't you too behave like a child now. And come into the house!'

'Hey look!' Dunu pointed at the coconut.

The knocking had now completely stopped and in its place, a fizzing noise commenced. The coconut started swaying slightly, like a drunken man trying to walk. Smoke began to trickle out from the base of the coconut's stem. The fizzing noise gradually grew louder and louder, as if the spout of a giant kettle was letting off great tornadoes of steam.

'That's that!' Hazel would have no more of this mystery that gave her the goose bumps all over. She lifted Dunu with one hand, motioned to Grandpa to follow her with the other and started walking briskly, at times breaking into a run, towards the house. 'Follow up, Brum boy!' she barked at the dog without stopping.

'But, Hazel, that coconut!' Dunu protested, kicking her feet. Grandpa, however, knew better than to oppose Hazel in such situations. So he followed her like a lamb, though turning back every now and then to try to see what was the mystery sealed in that big nut.

'Hazel, please!' pleaded Dunu. She wanted to stay on and watch but had to give in to Hazel. So, she just turned around and shouted at the oowii-oowiis.

'Hi there! And I am Dunu. Friends?'

The three looked at one another.

'Friends!' they shouted back.

The oowii-oowiis remained standing by the coconut but their gaze followed Hazel and her team, till it was unceremoniously whammed as the door of the house swung shut upon their gaze, with Brum, Hazel and the Umatas inside it. So the gaze that followed them returned to rest upon the coconut that was now shaking tremendously. And as the oowii-oowiis stared at it, forgetting even to breathe, the stem fell off the coconut and through the opening thus caused, a dense grey blob of smoke, in size a little bigger than a fist, whooshed out from the coconut with great force!

4

Jerutu

With the speed of a hurricane, the smoke ball flew up to Ronie and hovered in front of his beak for a mere moment. Taken aback, a 'pwkaak' escaped the rooster. This greatly shocked the smoke ball, and it retreated once again, at tremendous speed, towards the coconut. But just as it was about to squeeze itself back into the big nut, it changed course and whizzed right up to the squirrel. It arrived at the squirrel's nose with such tornadic speed that Sunny's thatched roof stood up heavenwards on its roots, like an open umbrella suddenly closing the wrong way.

'Sandie, look! Did you see that?' Ronie whispered after he regained his wit. 'Did you?'

'That them blob o' smoke a-resemble, Sunny? While it be hovering near him squirrel? I did! I did! But me thinking that be illusion me alone see!'

'It wasn't an illusion, Sandie, it wasn't!' Ronie gasped.

'It wasn't!' Sandie repeated and suddenly turned white from pink, out of fright. The ball of smoke was now directly in front of her, making every attempt to look like a spider. It was trying to form limbs coming out of its gaseous mass. But the smoke in the limbs wouldn't hold form, they just blotted and dissolved.

'Hey, wait a moment then!' Ronie suddenly wondered aloud. 'Did it even look like me when it was hovering above me? Did it, Sunny?'

'I honestly thought it did.' The squirrel looked dazed.

'Note, then!' Ronie proclaimed. 'So this thing can take any form it wishes to. That means it has life! Boy! It's alive!'

'Hey! What are you?' Ronie asked the blob of smoke in great excitement.

There was just moving gas for a reply.

'You be them one o' some ghost?' Sandie asked.

Moving gas again.

'Or some ghost's fart?' Sunny asked with a sway of his fluffy behind.

More moving gas.

Sunny laughed at his own joke and raised a paw for Ronie to clap with one of his. A high-five. The mass of gas stopped fidgeting. Facing Ronie and Sunny, it seemed as though the gas observed the high-five movement intensely. 'You can talk? Or at least understand what we say?' Ronie asked.

Moving gas again.

'Er, well, looks like you can't talk. Any other way you can express yourself?' Ronie asked again.

In reply, the gas formed into a paw and gave a high-five splat on Ronie's face!

'Whoa! Okay, that didn't hurt! So, I take it, we're friends, right?'

There was relief and enthusiasm in Ronie's voice as he made an offer for friendship. Next, Ronie offered a claw for the smoke blob to clap on. The smoke blob once again formed into a paw and slapped Ronie's claw, but unable to stop its inertia, it dissolved past the claw.

'It's ... now where is it?' Ronie swirled around looking for it.

But the smoke blob had vanished.

～

The sun lazily peeped out from behind the mountains and its first rays shone brightly upon the golden stupa of the Dendup Gompa, far from the Umata farm, atop Mount Swrang. Exhausted from a sleepless and greatly exciting night, the oowii-oowiis trudged to the bottom of the oak tree. They decided to wait there for Owl to return from his night jaunt, to tell him about the smoke blob. The three had just slumped at the base of the big oak and leant against its trunk, yawning and stretching, when Owl's frantic flapping made them jump up with a start. Owl had only entered his home, but he flew right out again, absolutely stunned and almost falling down, despite his wings.

'Smoke! Holy Smoke!' Owl screamed as he gyrated up towards the sky, and then back down towards the oowii-oowiis, screaming all the while. 'Smoke! Mist! I don't know what! But it's pretending to be an owl! It's pretending to be me!'

Ronie, Sunny, and Sandie nervously hopped after Owl, searching for whatever had frightened Owl. There was nothing. They all tried to calm their limbs, though their hearts were still thumping rapidly. And just when all four stretched down upon the ground to catch a breath, they noticed they were not four, but five. The blob of smoke too had parked itself beside them. It stayed still when they did and moved when they did.

'I suppose this mass of smoke to be a soul,' Owl observed aloud, making as little movement as he could.

'A harmless one I hope,' Sunny whispered.

'Up at the Dendup Gompa, Old Monk calls them Jerutu. It may be a good spirit, or a bad spirit. Or a plain mischievous one. But a Jerutu, it sure looks like,' Owl recollected.

'How you be a knowing about this Old Monk, Owl? And this soul him be calling Jerutu?' Sandie asked.

'Ah, it was so, Sandie, that I flew up to the Gompa one night. As I sat there, lost in the dreamlike serenity of the place, I didn't realize how the hours went by. It was only when the sun rose on the mountain peak and light swathed everything around me that I realized, I would not be able to fly back home. I should have, while it was still dark. But the place was so alluring that I forgot myself. So, then fearing I would lose my way in the daylight and dash against some rock face, I settled on a branch of a majestic tree and stayed there all day waiting for dusk to fall so that I could return home to my oak.'

'What majestic tree was that, Owl?' Ronie asked.

'The Tree of Emancipation.'

'Tree of Emancipation! Fancy name, eh, Owl. What kind of a tree is it?' Sunny asked, still sitting very stiff.

'No ordinary tree, this Tree of Emancipation,' Owl explained, 'it stands right across the main door of the Dendup

Gompa, facing the glittering brass statue of the Buddha inside. It is believed, oowii-oowiis, that this tree had acquired as much enlightenment as Old Monk himself, from all its years of watching the Buddha and listening to the prayers of the monks.'

A collective but hushed 'Wow!' rose from the oowii-oowiis.

'It was under this tree that Old Monk sat during the day and gave discourse to visitors and younger monks.'

'What be them this course, Owl?' Sandie stretched a few limbs.

'Discourse, pretty lady, discussion. Talks. He spoke wise things about karma, about birth, rebirth, and the soul's ultimate deliverance,' Owl elaborated, 'and it was upon this tree that I had to wait the whole of that day. As I did so, I felt a deep sense of peace and wisdom seep into my ignorant being as I got to hear every word Old Monk had said that day.'

'You are not by your body but by your soul, by the spirit inside that body,' Old Monk had said as Owl listened that day. 'The spirit never dies, it only moves on from one body to another. The body is, therefore, the temporary home of the spirit, the soul. In the course of this journey from one body to another, for that brief moment when it is without a body, it is exposed to all the auras of the Universe.' All the young monks, whom Old Monk called lamas, had sat still and quiet, listening to every word with great reverence and attention. There were a handful of visitors from the neighbouring hamlets too. 'So sometimes the spirit may be brushed by an evil aura and sometimes by a good one.' Old Monk draped his shawl closer, for the mountain breeze was biting. 'It is for this reason, the influence of this aura, that the same soul behaves differently in different bodies, in different births. And this is the reason why prayers are said over the dead, to cleanse the soul of all evil influence and prepare it for the subsequent association, until its final deliverance. Now you may ask, if man wants the soul of the dead to rest in peace, to attain moksha, as they pray during the last rites, why does man also believe in the rebirth of the soul? Knowing that rebirth is not eternal peace for the soul, but nirvana is?'

'So then why, revered Old Monk, does man believe in rebirth?' a visitor had asked.

'It is so, kind woman, that until and unless a soul has fully repented for all its wrongs, it will keep coming back to life, in some form or another. It will keep on receiving opportunities for atonement. This explains rebirth.' The listeners nodded with immense wonder at Old Monk's wisdom. 'When the soul has atoned wholly, it is then ready for eternal peace. For Nirvana.'

A few small lamas brought in kettles of steaming herbal tea and poured it out into small bowls. A few more lamas took these bowls around among the listeners. One of them bowed in front of Old Monk and offered him a bowl.

'Ah! Thank you, my little Dechen!' and with immense childlike delight, Old Monk immediately sipped from the bowl, before resuming his discourse.

'And then there are souls which have lived in animal and insect bodies, whose last rites upon their death were not performed. What about them?' Old Monk asked, but went on to answer himself. 'So it is for these souls, whose last rites were not performed, that the Tree of Emancipation stands. If a restless soul can find its way to this tree, the Buddha's radiance on it and the reverberation of incessant chants and prayers of the monks around the tree unfailingly free the soul from its imminent journey to purgatory. But, and most importantly, never force the course of destiny. We mortals don't realize it, but the use of force to go against the designs of the highest powers, to chalk out our destiny, only aids the designs which are preordained by that power. For, that which is destined to be, will yet be.'

Sitting under the oak, the oowii-oowiis found Owl's narration of Old Monk's sermon as absorbing at that moment, as did Owl during that entire day at the Dendup Gompa, sitting on the Tree of Emancipation.

'Upon this tree await ninety-nine enlightened souls,' Owl heard Old Monk say that day, 'they all have served their purpose on earth to the full. Their souls have no more to repent and have been cleansed by the prayers at the altar of the Buddha. So now they shall attain deliverance on the night of Vesak Poya, when the moon is at its brightest, in the month of Baisakha. Just listening to the prayers and chants prepares them for this mystical, final moment.'

What Owl heard that day was Old Monk's soothing words, floating above the rhythmic drone of chants from inside the prayer hall in front of him and the hum of rotating prayer wheels from the east and the west of the Gompa. Also, from all around, a pacifying chime engulfed him. Owl didn't know what it was, but it seemed like a hundred wooden wind-chimes were being caressed to a gentle sway by the pure mountain breeze. Though this chime brought him profound bliss, it also scared him. Because it seemed to have reached within his soul only to find out if it was ready for salvation, or so Owl got the hunch. And Owl wasn't yet ready to part with his soul! Moreover, Owl had only heard the surroundings, he hadn't seen them. For it was day. Even if he would have, he probably would have kept his eyes shut, to let the power of the whole ambience raise his little being into the vastness of the Universe, into enlightenment.

The oowii-oowiis listened to Owl without once interrupting, without moving. And beside them, the mass of smoke too sat still.

'Do you be thinking that this,' Sandie gestured to the blob of smoke next to them with as little movement as she could and only rolling her eyes towards it, 'be a runaway soul from among them ninety-nine on that the Tree of Emancipation?'

'Maybe, maybe not. But it is a lost soul all the same. Only Old Monk will be able to tell us what should be done with it,' Ronie replied thoughtfully, 'maybe we should go and meet him.'

'Righto then!' exclaimed Sandie, bouncing off the ground, suddenly forgetting all about the smoke blob, on hearing about an adventure trip. 'Let us all be a-climbing Swrang Peak to Dendup Gompa. And who be craving them honour to give here pink lady a piggyback ride up the mountain?' she said with another bounce. Immediately, the blob of smoke made many more bounces and got elongated, stretched and bloated.

'Oh hell! We forgot the soul!' Sunny said. 'We can't climb Swrang Peak with that thing gassing around us.'

'Let us be leaving it behind,' Sandie suggested.

'Oh yeah? With whom, Smarty Pants?' Sunny retorted with a flick of his thatched roof.

'Wait, not just as yet,' Owl advised. 'The Gompa is far from here and we are not even definite whether Old Monk will know about this particular soul. It may just be a soul in sojourn.'

'If it is so, do you think it will go away on its own if we just let it be?' Ronie asked.

'It just as well may. But Ronie, friend or no friend, we cannot harbour a soul,' Owl explained, 'this, in all likelihood, is not the place for it to be. It must belong elsewhere, I suppose.'

So in the days that followed, whenever and wherever the oowii-oowiis roamed about, they always started out as three but when they rested by a rock, or stopped by the stream, they suddenly became aware that they were not three but four. The mass of smoke was always with them. They tried to run away from it. They tried to scare it away. They even tried to hide from it. But the smoke blob always caught up with them. However, there were rare occasions when it wasn't around with them. Those were moments when the oowii-oowiis heaved a sigh of relief.

'Foowoo! It's gone!' Sunny said on one such occasion when they felt relieved sitting by a rock, just the three of them. There was no smoke making up the fourth member. Ronie cautiously looked sideways, then turned his weather-cocked head in jolting movements to look every other way to see if the smoke blob was following them from some unperceivable corner. It wasn't.

'At last!' he sighed.

'It really be a gone this time, boys, gone it be, gone it be, smokiti shkookumbee!' Sandie sang, with a jig on all her tens.

The oowii-oowiis sat there for long, basking in their regained freedom. There was no sign of the smoke blob. They eventually arrived at the conclusion that it was indeed a stray soul that had wandered into the Umata farm and after a brief sojourn there, had gone its own way.

'Thank God!' Sunny said, his voice relaxed, 'no more gassy issue, no more heavy stuff like salvation and stuff about the Universe. Because I need all my brains...'

'Ho! You be having them?' Sandie giggled, shaking all over. Sunny plainly ignored her and went on.

'...and brawns to crack my own good stuff.' And saying so, he picked up the nut that he was holding, one with a very hard shell, and raised it high with a paw to bring it down with great force upon the rock. But when the nut landed on the rock, it landed like an aircraft that had crashed and caught fire. Heavy smoke was trailing behind it. The smoke blob! It had trailed after the nut, back to the oowii-oowiis.

Bewildered, Sandie let out such a terrible squeal that it shook many pine cones off the trees. Ronie's wings opened out on their own in shock. And Sunny shook his paw violently and blew onto it as if it was the paw that was on fire. His nut rolled away into the thickets, never to be found and eaten.

'Enough of it!' Sunny fumed, when they all regained their composure. 'Let's just stop running away from it and instead try to make it run away from us. Show it how to fly, Ronie.'

Ronie obediently started a trot down the narrow foot track through the wild, grass flowers, gathering momentum before flapping out his wings and taking to a flight.

'Hey look!' Sandie screamed. 'It truly be a-trying to follow Ronie!' and she bounced up and down flaying her limbs all about her, glad at the thought that the soul, if at all it was one, would now hopefully fly away and be gone for good.

'Stop distracting it, Pinky!' Sunny scolded her, and with a swish of his fluffy tail, brought Sandie upon the ground and held her there. 'Just let it fly away, girl!'

Somewhere in a distant peak, an eagle squawked. 'Stop laughing!' Sandie grumbled at it.

However, the smoke blob could not fly away. It wasn't even anywhere close to a rooster's pitiful flight. It just about managed a very pathetically short distance before slumping upon the ground into a pool of smoke. This left the oowii-oowiis greatly puzzled. Sunny tried to teach it how to hop away but the smoke blob could not do that either.

'Strange, Owl,' Ronie said later that evening, as they all gathered around the oak, 'aren't souls supposed to fly and move great distances through every possible element? Why this, then? Have you noticed that our blob of smoke cannot fly even for a short distance without melting onto the ground?'

A gentle breeze rustled through the mighty oak, softly fluffing up a few feathers on Owl's white wings. The breeze was nature's way of assuring Owl and the oowii-oowiis that air ought to move, up the mountains and down the valleys, through trees that dressed the slopes and brooks that bathed the hills. And not plonk upon the ground, like the soul hanging around with them. It was also nature's way of telling them that hence, it was no ordinary soul.

'Yes, while I notice so, I don't understand the reason behind it,' Owl doubted his wisdom, 'because all other souls can move over great spans of space and time.'

'Poor us! Carefree days are over!' Sunny moaned, bringing his thatched head into his paws. 'Poor me!'

'Wait, Silly!' Sandie said, slapping Sunny's thatch roof, 'it just may be some a-kind o' different sort o' soul. It be a-wishing to stay with us or be a-trying to take us some else a-place! Might not it, Owl?'

Owl thought hard.

'Else a-place, as in?' Ronie didn't think Sandie was being silly this time. 'The Gompa?' he asked.

'Me not a-knowing,' she replied.

Then on, Owl and the oowii-oowiis gave up their efforts to get rid of the blob of smoke. Instead, they made plans to put it back into Owl's hollow to keep it from bothering them while they decided whom to ask about what to do with it. So it was decided that during the day Owl would guard it so that it wouldn't escape, and during the night the oowii-oowiis would take turns in sitting at the mouth of the hollow, guarding it.

'However,' Owl shut his eyes and spoke, 'this can only be a transitory arrangement. It cannot go on forever. You see, it has already been more than a fortnight that the soul has been with us. The only way out I see is to seek Old Monk's help. He may know about this sort of unique soul or he may not. It may be one of those ninety-nine Jerutus, or it may not be. Whatever it is, Old Monk is the only person I know who shall be able to help. And if he can't, I can only hope that he will at least be able to tell us about someone else who can.'

'Then we'll eventually have to go to the Gompa?' Ronie asked.

'Yes.'

'Okay, but please, I am not the one to stay back to take care of Mr Gas!' and Sunny stepped a few paces away from the group which was in the midst of a meeting of great importance.

'Eh … actually … me be a little scared, Owl, of staying all alone with them a somebody with no body,' Sandie hesitantly expressed her own reluctance.

Ronie stayed quiet.

'None of you need to stay back, oowii-oowiis,' Owl settled the matter for them, 'for all of you need to go to the Gompa.'

'Whoa!' Ronie found his voice, 'how's that possible? Who looks after Mr Gas then?'

'Go to the little girl in the house there,' Owl advised, 'meet her, and meet her fast. Ask her to look after the soul while you are gone. It is an enormous task to keep that thing still. If we lose track of it and lose it, the poor thing will be deprived of reaching its rightful destination.'

So it was decided that the oowii-oowiis would go and meet Dunu. But their immediate concern was to put the blob of smoke into Owl's hollow, which in itself was a task as enormous as going to the Gompa, leaving the smoke blob behind. Thus began a noisy deliberation as ideas, plans, approvals, and general disapprovals darted to and fro among the oowii-oowiis and Owl.

'Okay, we just blow the gas into the hollow, don't we?' Sunny thought aloud.

'Hah! As if it's that easy!' Ronie disapproved.

'If only we could make it understand what we said,' Owl rued.

'How about making a loud noise and scaring it?'

'Tsk! Tsk! No, no, no!'

'How about singing a lullaby, putting it to sleep and then transferring it into Owl's hollow?'

No plan seemed to look like it would work with the spirit.

'Wahei missy!' Sunny nudged Sandie with his tail. 'Why so silent? No ideas up that pretty pink head?'

'Me been a-thinkin, and thinkin good and smart.'

Saying so, she didn't wait for approval. She just went ahead and made slow but obvious movements of crawling into Owl's hollow. The rest of them fell silent and sat still, wondering what she was up to. Seeing her move towards the hollow, the mass of smoke whooshed into one mini-spiralling hurricane, and in no time was inside Owl's home. Just as Owl and the oowii-oowiis had hoped for.

'Bravo, girl! Bravo!' Ronie flapped a wing on Sandie.

Owl quickly moved in after the spirit and positioned himself at the opening of the hollow. He fluffed himself up, blocking the entrance and holding the smoke in with him. Only now could the oowii-oowiis move away.

'Ahaa! What a luxury this is! To breathe freely and move without fear!' Sunny rolled on the ground, catching a few grass flowers that stuck up his thatched hair. They stretched and flexed their limbs as if they had been cooped up in a sardine can for ages, before moving out to look for Dunu.

In all this time, a few more days and nights went by. The full moon, upon which the mass of smoke arrived at the Umata farm, began to wane until it disappeared, only to reappear like a thin smile upon the Kindoree night sky. Now it was starting to swell again. The oowii-oowiis and Owl went through anxious times, watching over the smoke blob as well as being on the lookout for Dunu all the while. All of them were losing out on sleep and being constantly on the alert was driving them crazy.

And then one noon, it looked as if a nap spell had been cast over the Umata farm. Brum lay on his back upon the grass just outside the patio with all fours spreading outwards and skywards, sunning his underbelly, his large head tilted to one side and the tongue sticking out. Ducks buried their beaks under a wing and pulled up a leg to rest on just one. Farmhands pulled their straw hats over their faces as they lay on shady patches to catch a quick nap. Even leaves on the oak were still. Up in the sky, not a bird flew past, and the lofty mountain stood watch like a doting parent. This sleepy calm reminded the oowii-oowiis that they hadn't had much sleep for quite a while now. Fatigue and anxiety sat so heavily on their eyelids that try as they would, they couldn't keep their eyes open. They collapsed to mere slits, giving each no better than a very narrow, horizontal view of the Umata farm. Suddenly, Ronie elongated his neck, fluffed up his plumes and let out an abrupt 'kawkrokk awk kkawk' that pierced through the tranquil afternoon.

'Aaw! You be shutting up now, Ron, and be getting some sleep!' Sandie shot back, startled.

Ronie did shut up but his call set off a whole chain of 'kawkrokk awk kkawk's from the domesticated roosters around the farm coops.

'Okay, but what was that for?' Sunny asked, his words slurred with sleep.

'Dunu! It's Dunu! She's back from school!' Excitement drove away the last winks of sleep from Ronie. He kept looking towards Dunu, lest they lost track of her.

'Shall we go and meet her? Right away?' Sunny asked.

'Yeah, no harm I suppose?' Ronie replied.

'No harm, no, no, no! Let's be a-go go go!' Sandie gave the verdict.

'Hop on up here then, Sandie girl and hold tight.' Sunny motioned to the spider to climb up his back and the oowii-oowiis sped across the quiet afternoon, hopping over sleeping snails and brushing past idling butterflies, to meet Dunu.

They felt the breeze upon their faces as they darted towards the little girl. The farm was slowly coming out of its noon siesta and birdsongs were once again filling the air. A clumsy beetle collided against Ronie's head as they raced across the farm, but they didn't let these distractions slow them. The poor spider was almost thrown back by the air rushing towards her with tremendous force. She had to desperately cling on to the squirrel's thatched roof with all ten limbs, as she flew through the air, a few inches above Sunny's head. She looked like a pink balloon tied with more than one string to the squirrel's neck. Ronie and Sunny ran with such speed that when they neared Dunu, which they did sooner than they had expected to, they found it absolutely impossible to put on their brakes and slow down decently. Instead, they just managed to come to an abrupt and screeching halt, almost crashing into her. This resulted in Sandie being unable to control her inertia of motion and was thus catapulted right on to Dunu's shoulder with such a heavy, noisy *whamp* that the little girl screamed in terror.

'Eeekk! Hazel!'

And in an instant Hazel was beside her, like magic.

In the next instant, Hazel's mouth opened wide and her eyebrows bounced up to touch her hairline. She let out a seemingly very high-pitched shriek, but which mercifully turned mute seeing two of the oowii-oowiis at a belly-nudge away. She hadn't seen the spider because Sandie had by then stealthily crawled down Dunu's back into her school satchel and hid herself in there. Hazel, Dunu, Ronie and Sunny were all in a state of shock at the rapidity with which the whole event occurred. The rooster and the squirrel tried to hide a beak and a nose respectively from Hazel's view, hoping that would shield from her view the rest of their bodies as well. It didn't. So as a second option, Dunu quickly gathered her wits about her, swallowed the lump of nervousness hard that was stuck up her throat all along, and initiated an introduction.

'Er … Hi Ronie! Hi Sunny! This is, umm … Hazel.'

'Hey, she's a nut!' pat came Sunny's voice.

Hazel fumed.

'Look! Look at the audacity of that nincompoop,' she shouted, laying much emphasis on the last four letters, 'that running-short-of-brown-dye squirrel! He dares call me a nut!' She stamped the ground with a heavy foot with such tremendous force that the ground shook and the vibration thus caused raised Ronie and Sunny a thumb above the good earth. It immediately triggered a 'right-about-turn-and-flee' act in the two. An outraged Hazel pulled Dunu into the house after her. However, when Hazel was looking upfront towards the house, Ronie made a quick low flight back to Dunu from behind and whispered into her ear, 'Sandie Spider is in your school satchel. She needs to talk to you. It's important…'

Dunu had just enough time to nod at Ronie before the door between her and Ronie slammed shut. And she was in her room.

5

Back into the Nut

Hazel's endless, unintelligible reprimands gradually faded as she moved away from Dunu's room. Her curvaceous figure disappeared down the veranda, heading towards the kitchen, until her voice became no more than a high-pitched background hum. Inside her room, Dunu anxiously looked around, unsure where to hide Sandie Spider. It had to be a spot Hazel wouldn't think to reach— no eyes, hands, toes, or any part of her inquisitive body could discover it. And it had to be quick because, any moment now, Hazel would return with a mug of milk and a plate of cookies for Dunu.

'There, them drawers?' Sandie suggested, pointing at the chest of drawers below Dunu's wardrobe.

'No,' Dunu declined, 'Hazel will open them to put in my laundered socks and undies.'

'Umm … in the behinds of them books, on your desk?'

Dunu shook her head again. 'Not there. Hazel often clears the mess on the desk and while doing so, pushes the books towards the back. And if you're behind those books, you'll end up like a bowl of strawberry jam against the wall, all squashed and splat!'

They were running out of time, drowning in overwhelming anxiety.

'Okay then, how it be inside a shoe?'

'You won't fit in.'

'Up the curtain?'

'You'll slide down.'

'Me pretend me a-balloon?'

'She'll blow into you through the mouth and tie you up a maypole.'

They were still scrambling for a hiding place when Hazel's heavy footsteps began thudding closer to the room. Her voice, too, grew louder, cutting through the girls' rising panic.

'...And no more—no more of these beings of the dark in my house, young lady!' Hazel's words rang out sharply. 'Have you washed those hands of yours with soap? A rooster with a weathercock on his head—what nonsense! Can you even imagine that?'

'Hey yes! The bathroom, come!' Dunu picked up the spider and rushed into the bathroom just in time to prevent Hazel from seeing Sandie. Now wherever Hazel walked in the house, the thud of the wooden boards under her feet vibrated through the whole of the rest of the house. And Dunu, Grandpa, and Brum knew precisely where she was heading. Just so, now Dunu knew that she was entering her room. Rightly so. She entered the room, set the tray of milk and cookies on the table and walked out. She didn't look back but as was her way, she kept rambling continuously.

'Now come out fast from that bathroom and finish your milk before it gets cold. I need to go and check on Kelman. That boy! He always slices the pork too thick or too thin to be picked up with the fork. And Thapa, where are you boy? Don't you rake up the wrong patch of straw now. That is left for the mushrooms to shoot! You hear me?'

Inside the bathroom, Dunu put Sandie down gently on the rug beside the bathtub, kicked off her shoes and sat next to her, leaning against the tub and looking at the spider with absolute awe and adoration. And the spider did the same to Dunu.

'So, this is how them little girls be, eh? Like spring flower? Only with the filament growing there a-behind?' Sandie asked, looking at the ponytail. Then she rolled her eyes upwards to have a better look at her spring flower.

'Okay,' Dunu said, smiling, 'now that we're safe from Hazel, at least for now, tell me, Sandie, Ronie said it was important. So, what's important? And yes, what was that mysterious whiff of smoke? But hey! Look at you! You're just so am-ma-zzing! A pink, heart-shaped spider! You're actually huggable!'

'Ssh!' Sandie replied as a single answer to all those questions, lest Hazel came up and heard them. She crawled closer to Dunu and said almost in whispers, 'What be important is to say about that the mysterious whiff o' smoke that I be here for. Yeah, that forced its own self out o' that a-rolling nut, you do remember? The coconut? It be a mass of holy smoke!'

'A mass of holy smoke…?' Dunu's jaws dropped.

'And it be making itself to look like … like … just about them anyone,' Sandie thought for a moment and then added, 'but it does not have enough smoke in it to make itself spread out into that her whole, hassled Hazel!'

And they both giggled.

'It can be a spirit, like a jinni, said…'

'A Jinni! Golly Gimplink!' Dunu interrupted in a loud whisper, unable to hold her astonishment. But she soon covered her mouth with a hand because they heard someone walking into the room.

'O dear me! That milk is still standing there. And not a bite from those cookies!' Hazel had reappeared in the room, with Brum tottering after her. They could hear Brum sniffing at the bathroom door. 'Dunu, you still in that pee-poo place? Are you sick, child? Dunu?' Hazel worried as she started walking towards the bathroom door.

'Are you constipated, Dunu?' she asked with concern, sticking up an ear against the door.

Inside the bathroom, Dunu looked at the spider, confused and questioning. Sandie was now perched on the edge of the tub.

'Quick! Say yes!' Sandie prompted.

'Umm … ah … yes. Yes … Hazel, I am … er … constipated but not so much that you should worry about,' and she made appropriate noises to support her claim.

'Poor dear. My poor dear,' Hazel began to fret, 'by the time you are done with that, I'll go warm up the milk. It is for this that I keep telling you to down more and more of the juices and water. And lettuce with olive. But no! Grandpa would stick that lolly of mutton and that leg of chicken up for you to bite into.' Her voice trailed away. But they could still hear Brum, sometimes thumping his tail against the door and sometimes trying to shove his muzzle through the narrow slit under the door. After a while, he slumped upon the doormat and with the muzzle still shoved into that breather, he fell asleep waiting for Dunu.

'It is a soul,' continued Sandie, 'so Owl be saying. And it be a-scared of us and us be a-scared of it. Owl says it may either the good soul be, or the bad soul be, but soul it sure be. Owl wishes for help from you. You will help, won't you?'

Dunu's pulse was racing with excitement. A spirit in her very own backyard! She pinched herself. 'Ouch! Okay, I'm awake and it's true!' She looked at the spider. She too seemed straight out of a fantasy storybook.

'In what way may I be of help, Sandie?' Dunu asked enthusiastically.

'You be having to safe keep the jinni, be taking care of that soul. You be having to keep it from whooshing away. Which it keeps a-doing. It also a-moving with great speed, at the slightest of movement by them other things and beings near it.'

'Will I be able to?' Dunu asked, realizing that it wouldn't be as easy as it sounded.

'Will you be able to? Yeah, that be another matter. But shall you? Us oowii-oowiis be a-going up Swrang Peak, to visit Dendup Gompa. There be Old Monk. Us seek help of him to send spirit where it belongs,' Sandie replied, trying to sound wise.

'Oh, okay. I mean, I guess it should be okay. Well, does it mean I shall be in complete charge of a spirit? A jinni! Golly gimplink!' Dunu found herself twisting her fingers out of ecstasy. Her hands and feet were tingling. She didn't know if there was a twinge of fear as well in her. She suddenly remembered that Grandpa had once gifted her a book on jinns and supernatural beings. So, she ran out into her room to look for it. She recollected that in that book, there was a bit about how jinns behaved. Looking up that passage might help, she thought. The moment she opened the bathroom door, she tripped and fell over Brum. Getting up on her feet fast, she dashed for the bookshelf.

Once in her room, she hastily looked through the rows of books on her bookshelf. She tried to look for it as quickly as was possible, so that she could get back into the bathroom before Hazel reappeared. But Brum kept getting into her way. He also wanted to keep entering the bathroom, and Dunu had to keep pulling him back by the collar. As it had to happen, everything seemed to be working hand-in-hand to hold her back longer in the room. She was so engrossed in looking for the book that she didn't even realize when Hazel had reappeared and was standing right behind her.

'Now drink that milk before it gets cold again,' Hazel barked down her nape.

Hazel's voice startled Dunu. She turned around abruptly, dropping the couple of books she was holding.

'Oh! Hi Hazel! I mean…'

Hazel made Dunu drink the milk and eat the cookies right then and there, right in front of her, making her chew the cookies well and slow, and pushing them down her throat with the milk. A giant glob of drool stretched from Brum's mouth to the floor as he watched Dunu lap up the milk. So, she stealthily made a bit of cookie slip from her hand, allowing Brum to lick it up. 'Didn't Hazel really see that?' Dunu wondered as Hazel picked up the tray with the mug and the plate and walked out of the room, thinking aloud, 'If only those wild, marshuko roots behaved! I wouldn't have had to be after Joyan to dig them up and fling them far. But since they don't behave and have entangled and choked the whole lower row of radish ... hey Thapa! Not there, fool, higher!'

Just then Dunu realized that weird noises were beginning to emerge from the bathroom, noises that weren't there when she was inside. She felt grateful that Hazel kept talking to herself and hadn't noticed those strange sounds.

Dunu got alarmed and came hurrying into the bathroom. This time Brum too was at her shins. She didn't find the book though. She looked around the bathroom but couldn't find Sandie either. And yet, Dunu kept hearing some gurgling noise at intervals. She couldn't make out from where exactly the gurgles came. She looked into the bathtub, but it was empty.

Dunu heard a 'plonk' and checked the washbasin. There was nothing there.

A 'plonk' again.

She checked the outlet of the bathtub. Nothing pink was stuck up there either.

'Brum! Come on, help me find Sandie instead of just sniffing at the base of the pot! Please, ole boy, quick!'

Now she heard 'Glubg ... glok...'

This time she followed the sound and just as she was about to lift the lid of the pot and look inside, she heard Grandpa's voice in her room. So, she nervously put the lid back and stood as still as she could, scared even to breathe. Brum began to claw at the pot and tried to lift the lid with his muzzle. Out in her room she heard Grandpa looking for her and when he saw that she wasn't there, he let his booted feet carry his rotund self away. Dunu heaved a sigh of relief.

Brum had meanwhile reached up to the cistern with his forelimbs and in the process, the flush-lever got pulled.

Immediately, a faint voice from somewhere coughed. 'Don't … glogkhwapp … flush! Don't!' it gasped and coughed.

The voice made Dunu jump up and turn around. The water inside the cistern began to swirl noisily like a whirlpool.

'Down a-here,' the voice was almost choking, 'the pot…! Cough! Cough! The pot!'

'Sandie? My! My! You in there?'

'Oooah! Gllug gurgle…!'

Bewildered, Dunu quickly lifted the pot's lid and saw Sandie spinning in the swirling water—sometimes skimming the rim, other times nearly slipping down the drain. There was no time to grab gloves or pincers. With a desperate plunge, she thrust her bare hands into the pot and snatched Sandie out, just as the last of the water spiralled down the pipe.

'Golly Gimplink! Look at yourself!'

Brum was sniffing Sandie all over and even gave her a couple of nudges with his large paw.

'But how, Sandie? Dear me! Why … I mean, how on earth did you land in there?'

'Oh, me do a-investigate around the bathtub,' she said, still burping out large soap bubbles which Brum began to chase, 'checking out them cute floating rubber ducks, brushes and loofahs. And me help meself to an unguided tour of the entire bathroom as me wait and wait for you to return, Dunu, me a-wanting to go out there and see what a-taking you so long but me hear him big dog and Hazel's voice out there, so me know, it be no safe to go out. So, to keep meself from getting a-bored and a-falling a-sleep a-snore, me doing a-climb the rack above the bathtub and gingerly, very gingerly, a-crawl among them little ceramic pots and bottles, them that a-making your bath and body lotions. Me sniff a few.'

Dunu had meanwhile wiped Sandie with sheets of tissue and after making her sit on some more, she began to prepare a bath for her. Sandie continued to narrate her adventure, 'One dainty pink glass jar be having a short spout at the upper edge and it be smelling oooh-so-flattering,' and she closed her eyes lazily and breathed deep, recollecting that flattering smell, 'so me a-hop onto its rubbery top and a-bend me head forward as low as me could to peep in through the spout. As me a-doing so, me no aware that me heavy body a-press down onto the rubber pump of the jar.'

Sandie had just positioned and stuck one eye into the opening of the spout to look inside when suddenly the spout squirted out a creamy liquid right into that eye. Startled, she let out a loud 'Oooaah…!' and in the process, opening her mouth wide and big. And as her mouth opened, another squirt of that 'oooh-so-flattering' liquid had dropped right into her mouth from the spout.

The shock had made the spider lose her balance and she tumbled down, rolling down along the rack, right into the little pool of water in the poo-pot below. As she fell, she also brought down with her the lid of the pot from its upright position against the cistern, to rest along the rim of the pot. So, the pot was now covered, with Sandie plonked inside it like a fist of pink poop at the base, gurgling and frothing up the pot with fragrant soap bubbles. And that was how all the weird noise began.

'Dear me!' Dunu found her voice at last, 'so that's what you did to yourself to raise all that gloopityglug noise!'

Sandie smiled sheepishly and nodded.

Only after Dunu gave Sandie a nice warm bath did she stop feeling like poop, though she still looked like a drenched ball of pink knitting yarn. The girls were at last out in Dunu's room, ready for a discussion of grave proportions. Dunu placed Sandie on a corner of a soft towel on her bed and wrapped her with the remaining towel like a blanket. By way of discussion, it was decided that they would bring the spirit to Dunu and that she would look after it till their next plan of action.

'Oh! And please, don't let that your big Hazelnut be knowing of all o' what happened today and are about to a-happen in the coming times. It be that, er, what be that called? Ocean-crate?' Sandie told Dunu with the air of someone capable of rich vocabulary.

'Secret!' Dunu corrected with a glorious smile.

'O whatever. But that be it.'

'That be it!' Dunu repeated after Sandie.

Dunu hid Sandie in the frills of her frock and in the pretext of taking Brum out for a walk, she took Sandie out of the house to drop her at a distance from where she could crawl away to her friends.

And before darkness set in, the oowii-oowiis used the same trick once more, which they had earlier used to put the spirit into Owl's hollow, to put it back into its coconut. They then covered the coconut with a large leaf and Sandie spun a pink thread all around the middle of the nut in a way that the leaf would not fall off. Sunny gave the coconut, gentle shoves to let it roll towards Umata's house. When they were below Dunu's patio, Owl flew up to check if it was okay to knock at her door. When all was clear, Owl flew back up with Sandie on his back and when they came upon Dunu's door, he let her off. Sandie knocked on the door gently and by the time Dunu opened the door and Sandie explained about the spirit being put back into the nut and covered with the leaf, Owl flew down once again and came up, this time with Ronie.

Owl and Ronie worked together, each gripping one side of the coconut with a wing while flapping furiously with the other to keep aloft. With great care, they lowered the coconut onto the floor of the veranda, ensuring it landed gently before retreating with a sense of urgency. Dunu looked at the nut in as much bewilderment as in anticipation. Her little heart thumped loudly, and her fingers shook as she picked up the coconut.

'Golly Gimplink! A spirit in my hands!'

She hurried inside and gingerly positioned the nut upright, nestling its pointed end onto a small towel folded like a ring cushion to keep it steady. Once satisfied, she carefully placed it in the bottom drawer of her study table—the only drawer that could be latched from the outside. With the spirit securely tucked away, the oowii-oowiis exchanged glances of relief and determination. They were now ready to set off and meet Old Monk.

❧

Early next morning, the oowii-oowiis set out for Dendup Gompa. Sandie sometimes rode on Sunny's back and sometimes on Ronie's. They hopped across the breezy, open slopes of the Umata farm, past the row of poplars and rode over the swinging cable bridge into the winding mountain tracks. The sun warmed their coats and birds flew with them for a distance, before flying away up into the blue, cloudless sky. The oowii-oowiis realized that they had almost forgotten how it felt to hop about as and where they wished, climb whatever rock, tree or fence that caught their fancy and stop to rest wherever they felt like, because they had got so habituated to stay guarded with the smoke blob following them all the time. Strangely, they also realized that instead of enjoying the carefree lives they had regained, they were missing the smoke blob. Somewhere along their chase-and-run, the oowii-oowiis and Owl started to look forward to the smoke's super-startling, abrupt appearances.

'Uh, well, boys?'

'Hmm?

'Yes, Sandie?'

'Well, be nothing. Just like that.'

They continued quietly.

'Me hope him smoke be a-fine and safe.'

'Missing the smoke blob, right?' Ronie asked.

'Of course not! Why me miss that a-smoke?'

'I just thought so. Because I do,' Ronie replied.

'Sunny?'

'Oh, let me think, let me think, yeah! I'm done thinking!'

'So, what have you thought?'

'I've thought,' Sunny tried to lighten the moment, 'that I do indeed miss the smoke blob…'

'See!' Sandie jumped lightly on Sunny's back. 'Me knew it!'

'Whoa! Whoa! Sandie girl! Now listen up first! So, I said I do miss the smoke blob, but only, and only, because it appeared from a nut. *Only* that. And I love nuts. That's all. *Only* that!'

'He be a-cute, though!' Sandie at last admitted. 'Guess me miss the gas.'

They didn't exactly realize since when they started feeling so, but now they felt a kind of concern for it, a comforting kind, that made their hearts swell with love and care for the vulnerable mass of smoke. They hoped it was safe. And they went ahead on their mission of reaching the spirit back to its home, their hearts filling with more love for it with each passing moment. They would take till sundown to reach the gompa.

6

Reminders from the Past

Among the oowii-oowiis, Sunny Squirrel was the most familiar with the ridges, the tracts, and the mountain trees that lay along the path to Dendup Gompa on Swrang Peak. Though Swrang Peak wasn't far as the crow flew, the journey was anything but simple. For the oowii-oowiis, who hopped, walked, crawled, and sometimes swung from web strings, the uphill road seemed distant and treacherous. Yet their excitement about the journey and its purpose filled them with energy to tackle the laborious trek. Strange sounds echoed around them, making the forest feel alive. As they climbed higher, the undergrowth thinned, and the towering mountain trees shed their wide canopies. Instead, they rose straight and tall, with sparse, spiky leaves, as if striving to touch the peaks. The wind whistled sharply through the branches, accompanied by the occasional screech of falcons above and the roaring rush of unseen torrents plunging into the abyss below. Wild mountain goats nimbly scaled rocky faces as though they were meadow paths, while yaks grazed lazily, and insects created a lively cacophony of sound. Occasionally, a stone would dislodge and tumble downhill towards them, sending the group into a frantic huddle. Each time, they managed to avoid both the rolling rock and the risk of tumbling down the slope themselves. Every step demanded caution, filling their hearts with a mix of anxiety, yelps, and the occasional giggle. Despite the challenges, their spirits remained high. Suddenly, Sandie burst into a sprightly, bouncy song, and the others quickly joined in, their voices echoing through the mountain air, turning the arduous climb into a joyful adventure.

A-swing, a-skip, a-swing, a-hop-aa
Old Monk to seek and meet,
Up and up to Dendup Gompa
We race so none can us a–beat.
O—o—o to Dendup Gompa...
We're off to the Gompa!

Tiny bugs on mighty mount,
Mighty mount of specks of soil
Wild pretty blooms abound
'n' no smoke to play a-spoil
O—o—o to Dendup Gompa...
We're off to the Gompa!

Hoppin' o'er frothy brook
With butterflies a leg we shook
Yet scared of falls and broken bones

Save our heads from tumbling stones.
O—o—o to Dendup Gompa...
We're off to the Gompa!

A-swing, a-skip, a-swing, a-hop-aa
Up and up to Dendup Gompa
We a-goin to the Gompa
Ronie, Sunny, Sandie Spidah
Us off to the Gompa!
Ye ye! to Dendup a-dup a-Gompa!

Just then, a sound interrupted their song, bringing them to an abrupt halt. It was the heart-rending cry of a small bird, echoing from somewhere high among the boughs. The anguish in that cry was so palpable that Sandie was certain it could only be a mother mourning for her children.

Sunny quickly traced the sound, his sharp eyes scanning the trees above. Without hesitation, he climbed up the trunk of the nearest tree, his movements lithe and silent. The cry grew louder as he approached, and soon he spotted the source—a restless, distraught mother bird perched on a branch. Her anxious gaze was fixed downward, so consumed by worry that she didn't even notice Sunny crouching beside her.

Following her gaze, Sunny saw what had caught her attention—a tiny, fragile tuft of feathers lying on the ground amidst the rocks and bushes below. It was a baby bird, weak and helpless. The only sign of life was the faint rise and fall of its chest, barely perceptible but enough to stir a pang of concern in Sunny's heart.

Her baby, yet unable to fly, had fallen to the ground. It had fallen from the nest and an old, starving snake was looking at it hungrily from a distance. The snake would have eaten it by then had the bird's mate not tried to distract and scare the snake so frantically and courageously.

'Oh hell! Ronie! Sandie! There's a snake trying to go for the fledgling!' Sunny alerted them, still perched up on the bough.

'Fledgling? Where?' Ronie asked, looking around him.

'There! Look over there, on the ground! Near the bush with the white flowers, the ones that look like trumpets!' Sunny said, directing them to the base of the bush with the fledgling.

Except for the serpent, none of them knew the white, trumpet-like flowers to be the Datura flower.

'Get together! Quick, do something!' Sunny said with urgency in his voice.

Instinctively, Sandie crawled as fast as she could towards the fledgling and placing all her ten limbs around it, raised her pink self above the little bundle of feathers. The fledgling now looked like it lay protectively under a miniature shelter, standing on ten pink, miniature pillars. The mother bird circled her nest once, to look at her other babies in it, before flying down to the one on the ground. Her mate continued to hover above the serpent, creating as much of a clamour as he could. As Sandie protected the baby, Ronie flew above the reptile to pick it up with his claws and drop him safely somewhere else, away from there. The serpent resisted and hissed back furiously, before slithering up the Datura bush. Ronie partly ran and partly flew after it. The mother bird's mate agitatedly darted about the bush and Sunny too joined them now.

In the scuffle that followed, much of the Datura flowers and leaves got crushed. And slowly, a strange smell began to emanate from the crushed flowers and leaves of the Datura bush. The smell, unsettling yet desirous, seemed to ease out their senses. The serpent alone knew that he had to get away from this smell before it drove him to a state of delusion. He alone knew, too, that the intoxicating smell of the Datura would make each of them feel sleepy and induce them into a state of hallucination. The serpent curled the tip of his tail around the last unspoilt Datura flower and plucked it with care. Thereafter, he held it there securely and let himself be caught under Ronie's claws. With the serpent held firmly in his claws, Ronie flew away from there as high and fast as his pitiful flight permitted him to soar. He planned to drop it far away from the little birds. Sandie and Sunny waited there for Ronie to return.

As Ronie flew with the snake in his claws, it sometimes wriggled to escape but mostly lay limp. Then it began to speak with great suffering, one that was induced by hunger and exhaustion.

'You have saved the bird, rooster,' it hissed with great effort, 'but in doing so, you have deprived me of my food. I am starving and am too old to look around for other prey. You have saved the bird but may kill me instead. So, tell me now, how is your deed justified?' he asked Ronie.

A cold shudder went through Ronie. He never thought of it from the perspective of the old, hungry and dying serpent. And he was sure, neither must have Sunny and Sandie. Were the oowii-oowiis truly justified in saving the fledgling? The words made him think hard before replying, 'But how do you know for sure that you would have got the fledgling, had we not arrived? You were anyway kept away from the fledgling by its father. His cries may have brought in more birds, which could have pecked you till you fled or even bled to…'

Ronie's vision was beginning to blur.

'Ah! Destiny!' groaned the old serpent.

And the word suddenly made Ronie hear Owl's voice, about what Old Monk told Owl.

That which is destined to be, will yet be…

'Do you realize that we might have even saved you? From the wrath of the birds?' Ronie was justifying the deed of the oowii-oowiis. 'We are not far from the Dendup Gompa. We can take you there with us if you think you can make it. We can arrange for some food for you there,' Ronie offered.

Ronie suddenly thought that he didn't feel the serpent wriggling in his claws any longer. Or were his senses numbing? Because his claws, try as he would, were no longer firm around the serpent. He also saw, in a blur, a kite hovering above them. Or was it an illusion? Scared that his failing senses may make the serpent fall off his claws and get hurt, he put it gently on the ground. But the moment he did so, the kite swooped down, snatched up the snake, and darted away. Startled, Ronie tried to follow the kite to save the snake. But a rooster whose senses were getting hazy could in no way match the flight of an alert kite. It surprised Ronie that deep in his heart, he felt sad for not being able to help the old serpent. But then, he also felt good that the baby bird was saved.

That which is destined to be, will yet be…

Ronie returned to the birds to find that the fledgling was already safe back in the nest. Sandie had tenderly lifted the tiny fluff of feathers on to Sunny's bushy tail and he carried it to the nest with the kind of care that he never remembered having bestowed upon anyone so far. He didn't even know that he was capable of bestowing such care. His heart felt strange. It was nervous and heavy when he was carrying the fledgling up the tree to the nest. But once he had carefully placed it among the other flightless fledglings in the safety of the nest, his heart felt amazingly light. There was a lingering taste of sweetness not on his tongue but in his heart. It ached with joy. And he thought he was in a trance.

'Could it be because of anything other than joy?' Sunny wondered.

The bird and her mate flew to the nest and in turns flew down to the oowii-oowiis, hopped around them a couple of times and flew back again.

'Me sure that a-hoppity skip of them mother and father birds be a thank-you ritual!' Sandie said, her voice choked with feelings she couldn't understand. But she wondered why she felt like she was swinging and swaying all the while on a web string!

Certain unforeseen events, and sometimes strange stupors, leave unexpected marks in life. The oowii-oowiis never could find out whether the mark left in their lives after that particular incident was a consequence of saving the fledgling as well as not abandoning the hungry, old serpent, or a consequence of the smell of crushed daturas intoxicating them. What was definite was that the boisterous oowii-oowiis seemed to have got drawn into a distant dreamlike phase, sucked into a profound whirlpool of life's truths. Their movements became clumsy and slow, the few words they spoke were slurred, and they felt like they had just woken up from sleep but would love to go back to it. They now moved ahead speaking not too many frivolous words, let alone singing and dancing. Whatever few words they exchanged, were words of great philosophy, of the ultimate truth that formed the basis of the universe. They felt serene within, having wished and offered to take the old dying snake to the gompa. They also felt peaceful for having saved a probable prey from its predator, and yet not abandoning the old, probable predator to starve and die.

But why did a sense of having done so, once upon a time, suddenly engulf the oowii-oowiis?

Meanwhile, late that same afternoon, the shrill cries of a kite pierced through the skies high above what was once Fhuwanji. But there was no one to hear that cry. For there was no Fhuwanji, nothing remained of it anymore. Had there been anyone there, he would have heard that cry and looked up. And then he would have seen a kite with a serpent held in its claws, hovering above the Bathou temple. He would have seen the serpent swoop down towards the temple and just before alighting on its decrepit roof, release the serpent from its claws. He would have seen the serpent drop with a gentle *whump* upon the ground just a few spans away from the shivling. With the white Datura still held carefully in the curl of its tail, he would have seen it slowly inch towards the shivling.

Had there been anyone there that afternoon, he would have seen Jeebou arrive at Bathou's altar, with the white Datura flower.

That moment, Jeebou could muster just enough strength, for just as long, to let his slimy body reach Bathou's stone incarnate. He then dropped down limp and long at the base of the shivling, consciousness driven away by fatigue. As Jeebou drifted into slumber, he awoke into a dream wherein the shivling slowly parted to let out rays of blinding orange light. And then a part of the light slowly turned into soft blue. A face with three eyes, the third resting vertically on the forehead, appeared amidst that soft blue light. Upon the head of that vision, nestled on a base of thickly knotted hair, rested the joukhoorei with a slight slant, dry and empty as ever. All three eyes were open when the face appeared. And as it often happened in dreams, Jeebou just knew the face to be Shiva's. His father's. Shiva had appeared to Jeebou to take an account of the tasks he had assigned Jeebou.

And Jeebou started to narrate a description of the completed tasks.

'Father, I had come across the Jataka creatures and put them to test…'

'And they have passed,' Shiva replied.

'I have brought you the white Datura…'

'You shall now place the Datura, your mother's powers, upon the shivling, at my disposal. And hence I close my two eyes!' Shiva told Jeebou.

And the face in the blue haze now had only the third eye open.

Strangely, in his dream, Jeebou felt no fatigue, no pain, no agony of the old and the exhausted. Neither did he feel energized with the vigour of the young. He simply experienced a state of complete bliss, where there was just nothingness. In his dream, he saw himself reaching up to the shivling and raising his tail with the Datura still cradled in its curl. Rays of light from Shiva's face fell on the Datura and it transformed into a splendid bloom, its whiteness attaining divine proportions. Shiva's eyelids moved with the movement of the white petal. As the flower opened wider and wider, Shiva's third eye got narrower and narrower. And when the flower reached its widest and most radiant bloom, Shiva's third eye closed completely.

'This fully open flower now remains at my disposal, Jeebou,' he heard Shiva speak to him, 'signifying your mother's vehemence. But the very light from me that has opened it to its fullest and most magnificent shall also scorch and parch it to a complete wither. And with that shall wither your mother's fury. Dwisikhlaa's force. The flower shall bloom again, only if I seek it to, only when I nourish it with my light.'

Even as Jeebou watched, still in a state of dream, the flower started to wrinkle and wither, just as the rays of light from inside the parted shivling started to wane and sink back into the base of the fissure. 'And the part of yourself that you had moulted at the base of the Datura plant, O Jeebou, which was your old skin, is but that aged and cursed part of you that you have already discarded,' Shiva continued to tell him, 'but you yet have a skin which is because you yet have a part of the curse that will stay on with you, though it will not make you feel old and aged. And now, slide away to your mother and remain there for all time, to surface, if ever, only when I command you to.'

Having said so, the face started to dim and shrink. But before it got sucked back into the parting of the shivling, Jeebou distinctly saw a trickle of jou flowing out of the mouth of the slanted joukhoorei, which was resting upon Shiva's head, to reach all the way down the shivling.

'Will there be fluid in the joukhoorei again someday? Has the soul of the joukhoorei been found, Father?' Jeebou asked Shiva in his dream. But Shiva's face in the blue light had already dissolved.

Jeebou didn't realize how long he lay there asleep. And when he woke up, everything around him was just as it was when he arrived there moments ago. The shivling wasn't parted, there was no light emitting from it. There was no face of his father's, no voice. Like it had been before, so was it now. He could see only abandonment and water all around him and could hear only the ripple of water nudging against more water and the flight of water birds far away. Jeebou felt his tail. He looked at it. The white Datura flower, however, was gone. He felt no fatigue, no vigour. He felt no joy, no pain. He only had a strong yearning to go back to his mother and remain curled there in her womb once again. And Jeebou did just that. He would uncurl and surface from there whenever and only if his father so ordained.

But there was no one at Fhuwanji to see that mystic occurrence that afternoon at the Bathou temple. When Creation desired to remain unchronicled, she left no witness. Not even the kite that destiny made to drop Jeebou was there. It had long flown away.

7

Dendup Gompa

Dendup Gompa was snugly nestled into the highest, snow daubed ridges of Mount Swrang. White chortens with golden steeples, as tall as seven feet as Ronie estimated, stood between the gompa and the Tree of Emancipation, but only along the sides. The space at the centre between the gompa and the tree was left without any barrier, for the tree to always have an undisturbed, whole view of the Buddha inside the gompa. Now of course, tiny prayer flags in yellow, blue, red, green, orange and white hung from long strings swinging from the steeple of one chorten to another, criss-crossing a part of the space between the skies and the earth over that central clear area. The grass on the ground was patchy and browned, a reminder of the mountain's rug of last summer, waiting to turn green once more. The winds that swept past the bright prayer flags carried the blessed chants of *Om Shanti* and *Om Mani Padme Hum* to wherever they blew, far and away. When the oowii-oowiis would reach the gompa and see from there the peak of Mount Swrang, they would notice snow still clinging on to the peak, though the severest of the winter snowfall would have long gone by. Some swore they had sometimes, on rare occasions, seen the snow there in the formation of a trident. Many even confirmed that they saw the snow trident on the same day when the villagers in the foothills observed shivratri, a night of prayers dedicated to Lord Shiva, Lord Bathou. That day there still was snow on the peak of Mount Swrang but it wasn't in any particular formation that could be seen as a sign from the Universe. That day the snow just sat splat upon the peak, all confused and not sure if that was the right place to be at that moment, just like the oowii-oowiis felt about arriving at the Dendup Gompa at that moment. Understandably nervous, the oowii-oowiis walked close together and followed the narrow rocky track that precariously lined the side of a steep crag. Cliffs rising beyond the ravine had more scraggy rocks and no more trees. The only scanty green that they saw was a seasonal cover of lichen. When the snow arrived, that too would all be gone. Monks from the gompa had cut branches of trees to erect crude but sturdy railings along the open edge of the track. Long, vertical prayer flags fluttering from tender shoots of mountain bamboo also lined the track on this side. Sunny had almost swooned when he tried to look down from the edge, leaning on the railing. He began to twirl on a leg and started screaming, 'Waaa! There's no ground below! Somebody save me! It's dark down there! I'm falling! I'm dying!'

'Shut up! Will you?' Ronie flapped him on the head and stopped him from swivelling and screaming.

The birds that hovered above them were no more the ones they would love to dance with. Instead, these were now falcons, hawks and eagles, that would love to carry the oowii-oowiis to their fledglings as supper. So whenever they heard a bird screech above them, they stuck their faces to the wall of the crag. Like nail to the finger. A roaring waterfall dropped hundreds of miles down the ravine to their right. When the wind got strong and blew in from the falls, it brought droplets of freezing water with it and sprayed the oowii-oowiis. Though Sandie shivered and grumbled about the chill that stung like pins, the moisture laden wind slowly re-stimulated their senses which were earlier numbed by the smell of the Datura. Whatever they saw and heard now, they did so as a reality and no longer as an illusion. They could at last see the stupa.

The oowii-oowiis had reached Dendup Gompa.

Ronie, Sandie, and Sunny gasped as they stood spellbound, losing themselves in the magic. Quiet and calm were never so powerful and never so all-pervading. Despite its physical smallness, the gompa created as much awe as did the majestic Himalayas on which it nestled, the way the stupa of the gompa rose above the highest grounds on earth into the vastness of the cosmos, leaving all things connected to earthly illusion, *Maya* as they called it, back at the base. There was now much life and activity in the gompa. Yet, all of it happened in such flawless synchrony and silence that it could only be compared with the life and activity of the planets along their physical orbits of time and space, and metaphysical cycles of truth and continuity. There was a row of wind prayer wheels on the western side of the gompa and a row of water prayer wheels along a creek on the eastern side. Even the infinite rise and fall of the hum of chants inside the gompa, and the clockwise spinning of the wind prayer wheels outside, retained amazingly precise timing and vibration. Monks explained that the breeze that made the prayer wheels spin, carried the essence of the prayers to all matter above the ground; and the waters of the brook that rotated the water prayer wheels carried the resonance of the chants to all matter beneath the ground. This brook came alive to cavort down crevices and ridges only when the snow in parts of Mount Swrang melted, around the month of Vaisakha. Around the time of Vesak Poya, it rapidly swam down, sometimes bouncing off rocks and sometimes tunnelling through them, to find its way down to the Umata farm and finally to join the Dwisikhlaa farther south. The brook had no name as such but because it brought blessings from the Dendup Gompa, they called it Dwisanchi in the plains. *Dwi*, which meant water and *sanchi,* which meant blessings. The snow on the peak yet remained, sometimes more sometimes less, but they remained all year through.

Now as the oowii-oowiis looked around the gompa, they heard a continuous hum of chants in the air. Small copper lamps of yak butter flickered around the chortens like timeless stars in the galaxy. In one section of the gompa, little monks were chanting over and over to learn by heart, the basic incantations of taking refuge and generating Bodhichitta.

SANG-GYEY CHÖ DANG TSOG-KYI CHOG NAM-LA
JANG-CHUB BAR-DU DAG-NI KYAB-SU-CHI
DAG-GI JIN-SOG GYI-PEY SO-NAM KYI
DRO-LA PEN-CHIR SANG-GYEY DRUB-PAR-SHOG.

Old Monk would later explain this chant to the oowii-oowiis as:

I take refuge in the Buddha, the Dharma, and the supreme Sangha,
Until I attain Enlightenment.
By the merit I accumulate from practicing generosity and the
other perfections,
May I attain Enlightenment in order to benefit all living beings.

Once the hallowed aura of the monastery completely seeped into their tiny beings, the oowii-oowiis slowly emerged from their daze and regained their speech and movement. Yet, they were still held in awe of everything around them. They took cautious steps upon those sacred grounds, lest they disturbed the balance inside the monastery, as they walked towards the main chamber. It was there that the brass idol of Buddha sat cross-legged in all radiance, his eyes closed yet seeing everything and every being. So much like Shiva.

'The sitting Buddha in there must be as tall as the standing Hazel in the farm!' Ronie whispered.

'Ssshh!' Sandie gestured, with a raised leg. Sunny dragged his tail along the grounds, forgetting about its existence.

And then the oowii-oowiis saw the Tree of Emancipation. It was everything Owl told them it was, and much more. Because they also saw what Owl had only heard, like the wooden wind-chimes. They saw that there were many of them and they were actually hollow pipes of mountain bamboo, with the closed end put earthwards and the open end facing heavenwards. These were looped onto fine yarns like those that a cobweb was spun with and hung upon the branches of the Tree of Emancipation. Only, the yarns glittered like threads of gold because of the light from the butter lamps that shone on them day and night. Whenever a soft breeze passed through them, the bamboo pipes swayed ever so gently, making the wind hum as they rubbed against the bamboo pipes. But the bamboo pipes never touched one another as they swayed, nor did they come in the way of one another. Because such is creation. There is always an interweaving link, like the breeze here, that blew in and out through all the bamboo pipes and touched each one of them while the bamboo pipes themselves never touched one another. Just as each being on earth lived through his own life, undetermined by another's, yet affected by the existence of others at some point of time, in some way or the other. And like the breeze, destiny spun through all of these lives as the interweaving link. The chiming pipes made the oowii-oowiis realize the truth of Creation, that it was all about the cycle of birth, death and rebirth, to step into the cycle with the only purpose of stepping out of it.

Gradually, dusk came to cloak the mountains. The winds and the cold grew more intense, and with it grew the number of flickering butter lamps. And Buddha looked even more resplendent. The oowii-oowiis stood under the Tree of Emancipation and watched Buddha, captivated and speechless. They stood there for long, immersed in the spiritual opulence of the surroundings. They didn't know why but they found the presence of the Tree of Emancipation strangely and greatly familiar, as if they had known one another from a previous birth. Each felt like they had all been together with the Tree and the Buddha during some very ancient time. And once again that same feeling of remorse rose in each of their hearts, like they had some time, somewhere, abandoned someone, to fulfil their own selfish needs, without being grateful for the care they had received.

Old Monk began his sermon early next morning, when even the sun hadn't risen. Draped in a maroon robe, he sat cross legged on a brightly coloured mat. However, the colour at the centre of the mat was faded, due to prolonged sitting upon it. He had a shawl of thick, yellow, yak wool falling from his shoulders and spread on his lap. The oowii-oowiis approached him slowly, with reverence and apprehension.

'The Jataka Creatures! I was waiting for you!' he said, as he saw the rooster, the squirrel and the spider approach him.

The oowii-oowiis were stunned.

'Reverence, Old Monk, did you know we were coming?' Ronie asked the moment he found his voice.

'Bathou told me in my dreams that you would come,' Old Monk replied.

'Eh...Bathou be who?' Sandie asked, almost apologetic that she didn't know who Old Monk was referring to.

'Bathou be the Lord,' Old Monk replied, the corners of his mouth breaking into a light smile.

'He also told you why we have come?' Sunny asked.

'Are you in search of the lost soul?' Old Monk only put another question as his response.

'Actually, we have already found one,' Ronie said, looking at the others for approval.

'*It* found us!' Sunny nudged Ronie.

'Whichever!' Ronie gave a stern look at Sunny gesturing him not to be disrespectful to Old Monk.

'But Old Monk, we don't know if it is the same soul as the one which you refer to.'

'Did it come out of fluid in a vessel?'

'No, no! Not at all! It not be come out of fluid in a vessel, Old Monk, it instead be a-whooshing out of that big nut, that green coconut.'

'Pretty lady, look at it as the universe does,' Old Monk explained Sandie, 'The universe sees the coconut as the vessel and the coconut water as the fluid inside the vessel.'

The oowii-oowiis exchanged approving 'ohs and 'ahs as they nodded at one another.

'So, is our smoke blob the lost soul?' Sunny asked.

'Does it travel far and long like other spirits do?' Old Monk once again replied with another question.

'It doesn't! And precisely that kept us wondering,' Ronie spoke with sudden excitement, 'it doesn't, Old Monk. It moves a short distance in amazing speed and then it goes slump! Like melted smoke spilling upon the ground.'

'Yes! Then it is the one! It is a Jerutu! We've found it at last! Yes!' Old Monk stood up instantly, ecstatic over having solved an age-old puzzle, 'we've found the Jerutu!'

'A Jerutu? Is that a jinn or a soul? Or a ghost?' Sunny wondered aloud.

'It is a spirit. A soul. One which is air like all other souls but which, unlike other souls, derives its energy from liquid. The soul is instinctively searching for, and is gravitating towards, the one thing or being with whom it shares a bond of long decades. It has lived long in the precincts of Shiva and thus has already been cleansed. That is why it need not have a sojourn in a prayer retreat like the other ninety-nine Jerutus. It is the last of the Jerutus, the hundredth. My adorable oowii-oowiis, do you see those bollongs?' Old Monk pointed above his head at the hanging bamboo wind-chimes without looking up, 'there are a hundred of those. Ninety-nine of them already have a Jerutu inside each, waiting to be liberated on the night of Vesak Poya, the night in the month of Vaisakha when the moon is at its highest and brightest.'

'However,' Old Monk continued as the oowii-oowiis listened in rapt interest, 'the Jerutus can be free only when all hundred of them are together in one place for deliverance. These ninety-nine have waited long, you see, they cannot be held back any longer than this Vesak Poya. They have been cleansed and readied for their emancipation. It is just the arrival of the hundredth Jerutu that we all await. If destiny wills, you reincarnated beings from the times of the Jataka will bring that last Jerutu here before Vesak Poya. Just in time for all the hundred Jerutus to be in their respective bollongs and at last attain emancipation. Nirvana we call it.'

If there was any feeling more overwhelming than enchantment, the oowii-oowiis felt it now.

'And if the hundredth Jerutu cannot be brought on time?' Ronie asked.

'We don't know as yet what will happen then,' Old Monk said with a calm in sharp contrast to the oowii-oowiis' excitement. 'If anything deviated like that is destined to be, it will yet be. But as of now, we are unaware as to what will occur upon such deviation. We are only aware of what will happen when the hundred Jerutus gather at one place at that final hour of Vesak Poya.'

'Wowittywow! That be almost like a story, Old Monk,' and Sandie could almost feel how a goose felt about its skin. 'Your mommy be reading this a-story during your a-bedtime?'

Thwack! Infuriated, Sunny slapped Sandie.

Old Monk smiled.

And as he did so, he added more wrinkles to his already

furrowed, adorable face. Also, when he smiled, his narrow slits of eyes became mere dark lines below his sparse eyebrows. Like the rest of the monks, Old Monk too had no hair upon his old head. But unlike them, he didn't have to shave his head. Because at his kind of age, hair just gave up on him. He was old, very old. And now he smiled. How blissful he appeared when he smiled, the oowii-oowiis thought.

'If that which is destined to be, the deliverance of the souls will take place.' Old Monk breathed long and deep, in anticipation of the days to come.

Sandie looked all around her and then looked up the Tree of Emancipation. Hundreds of small cocoons of soft, translucent yarn dotted the higher reaches of the trunk and the boughs. Sunrays danced into them as one colour but came out diffused as seven vibrant ones, making each cocoon look like a tiny piece from a rainbow.

'Awooo! That all be cater-posts in them a-cocoons?' Sandie was mesmerized. 'Them be waiting to turn to pretty butterflies? On the night of Vesak Poya again?' Sandie asked propping her pink self on four legs, two on either side of her heart shaped body, and moving the remaining six like a butterfly would flap its wings. Sunny and Ronie too looked up.

'They aren't cater-posts, little spider, not cater-pillars either!' Old Monk replied without looking up. Her manner of talking delighted him, so he imitated her, 'them not be cater-pillars. Them be Jaikhlongs.' They laughed. 'Every Jaikhlong is a retreat nest for those souls which once lived in the mortal bodies of lesser creatures like insects and worms, for whom there had been neither any prayers nor any rites when they left their mortal bodies,' Old Monk explained, 'hence, the soul had been deprived of eternal peace, of freedom from rebirth. So, the soul is reincarnated again and again, till the time comes when there are prayers upon it as it leaves a mortal body. Or, till its cycle of rebirth comes full. However, if during the transition from one mortal form to another the soul finds its way up here, then waves of prayers from the Buddha's altar wrap it securely against passing negative vibrations of the universe. But only if the purpose of its last birth had been served. These layers that form over every such soul in retreat are the Jaikhlongs. And let me tell you, oowii-oowiis, only prayers and blessings can penetrate the Jaikhlongs.'

Now Old Monk looked up.

'By this Vesak Poya, all of these souls will be ready for deliverance, and they shall be set free from their Jaikhlongs as well as from the cycle of rebirth. Little Spider, if you are here on that night of the Vesak Poya when the Vaisakha moon is at its highest and brightest, you too shall see that divine vision. Yes, at the time when all of them together float away higher and higher to merge into the mystery and power of the cosmos, they do look like butterflies, Sandie, butterflies made of tiny droplets of celestial light. Aah! How the sky illuminates at that moment! It will leave you bedazzled if you are here to see them.'

Old Monk knew they would be there to see them.

'And then again from the thirteenth day of the waxing moon, newer souls will come to rest on the boughs and trunk of the Tree, and cocoons of prayers will once more begin to form over them.'

'Ahm, Old Monk, you be excusing me please, but I be having this one a-doubt,' Sandie asked with gaining curiosity, 'if them souls be continuing to go away not to be returning to enter new a-bodies, then, Old Monk, will them living bodies on earth be growing less and less? And when all souls be going away, on what you say Nirvana, will there be no more of them a-creatures be living here on this a-earth?'

'You thought hard and wise, Spider,' Old Monk nodded. 'Yes, if there are no more souls to enter new bodies, how will new forms come to life? At the same time, the universe can never be left without any soul. There has to be souls to make newer beings come to life. And this will be when one mature soul divides into two and two mature souls further divide into four, like division of cells in the physical world. So, you see, just as souls continuously keep attaining deliverance from rebirth, new souls keep appearing to take their place in the mortal world. Like life in Creation. Just because there are deaths, it does not mean that life ceases. Because more lives are born to take the place of the dead.'

'So, er, the soul we found is the hundredth Jerutu?' Sunny asked.

'It is!' Old Monk replied.

'It has a bollong waiting for it up there?' Ronie asked, too amazed to believe.

'It does. It is unfilled now, but it will have its Jerutu soon, before Vesak Poya. And you will give this last bollong its Jerutu. The hundredth Jerutu.'

'And how do we do that?' Sunny asked.

'You will not do that. It will just come to happen; you will only be a medium. That which is destined to be, will yet be.'

'One more question, Old Monk,' Ronie asked, 'how many days do we have before Vesak Poya?'

'Four.'

'Four!' The oowiis-oowiis cried out in panicked chorus.

They started to sweat despite the cold, for there wasn't much time.

'Enough to get back to the farm and return with the last Jerutu,' Old Monk assured, as if reading their minds.

Old Monk's words put the oowii-oowiis into deep contemplation. How were they to bring Jerutu, who was air but drew sustenance from liquid, all the distance from the Umata farm at Kindoree, up Mount Swrang to Dendup Gompa, to the Tree of Emancipation?

The return trip down the mountain was a quiet one, each oowii-oowii deep in his own thought. Each was trying to figure out how to bring Jerutu up Mount Swrang. On any other day, just trying to make plans to transport Jerutu would have turned them into a boisterous group, each speaking to make its voice heard above the others. And more than half of the discussion would have been futile hilarity. But it wasn't so that day. They were sombre not so much from wondering how to fetch Jerutu but for being shown the truths of the universe which were sometimes unbelievably simple, yet at other times incredibly complex. Like Old Monk told them:

…If you stand and look up at the sky and beyond, you'll only see infinite nothingness. But when you look at that same nothingness after you have come upon the Tree of Emancipation, you'll see that it is that infinite nothingness which is the one and the only Power and Truth of the Cosmos. It is everything else that is actually nothing. Because all else is Maya … illusion…

Heavy thought for the fun-loving oowii-oowiis.

On their way back when they arrived at the place where they had saved the fledgling, they all instinctively looked up at the nest. The fledglings were perched on the branch outside the nest, learning to take their first unconfident flights. The mother bird kept watch.

'Look! They are learning to fly!'

The Datura plant was still bruised but there were signs of new buds and a few buds which got spared in the scuffle of a day ago were in half blooms. A long, stocking like molt from which a snake had crawled out, lay at the foot of the Datura bush. But now ants were feeding on it. All of it was a sign of resurrection, and the process of moving on. Because the powers of the cosmos shall let nothing come to a standstill, shall let no loss be mourned for long. Because creation never stagnates, never dies. It only resurrects.

Like Christ.

Like the Phoenix.

As of now, even the oowii-oowiis could not remain there for long watching the little bird. They had to reach Umata farm. They had work to do. Much work, and very less time.

8

Pholey Deehang

Pholey Deehang often undertook the long journey from his home, high in the forested hills of Bhutan, to the Bathou temple at Fhuwanji. His sons, brothers, and their families had moved even deeper into the hills, seeking livelihoods as hired hands. They cultivated land, chopped wood, grazed cattle, and carried loads as porters when needed, taking on any odd job that brought in money. Life was harsh, but it was life nonetheless—a stark contrast to Fhuwanji, where life had ceased altogether.

Fhuwanji itself had disappeared, swallowed by the relentless waters of Dwisikhlaa. As days turned into months and months into years, Pholey Deehang's family, along with many others displaced from Fhuwanji, rebuilt their lives in the forests. A new settlement emerged in the shadows of the hills, nestled near mountain streams and close to the plains that Fhuwanji had once called home.

These settlers had long abandoned thoughts of returning to their submerged village. The past lay buried beneath Dwisikhlaa, while their future took root in this rugged yet fertile land. Even if some miracle were to occur and Fhuwanji resurfaced one day, returning home would mean starting anew all over again—planting the smallest sapling, digging the ground to erect the first post for a house, and rebuilding every fragment of life from scratch.

Settling in the hills of Bhutan had already taught them, in the hardest way possible, what it meant to begin again. Back then, they had endured the trauma of being uprooted, both in body and mind, simply because there was no other choice. But now, after ten long years, they no longer had the strength to face such upheaval again.

A decade was enough time to adapt, to carve out a semblance of comfort under the challenging circumstances they had come to accept as their new normal. The thought of returning to Fhuwanji, even if it ever rose from beneath the waters, no longer felt like a dream worth chasing. It was, once, their home—but it had ceased to be.

In the ten years since the night of the devastating floods, Pholey Deehang had become a shadow of his former self—a man utterly wrecked by the memories of that fateful night. For him, time had frozen at the moment of the great deluge. No matter where he was, even in the high hills of Bhutan, he saw water everywhere, an unending tide of destruction that refused to leave his mind.

Often, in the dead of night, he would rise abruptly, consumed by panic. Gathering whatever he could find in the yard and stuffing it into a sack, he would rouse the others, urging them to flee as though the floodwaters were once again upon them.

'Go look out for Baulungbwrai,' he often whispered. When he was led back inside the house and made to sit down, he said, 'There is no time to sit, children, the waters are everywhere.' Sometimes, they even heard him talk to Girim Umata. Once tall and robust, Pholey Deehang's body had withered to a skeletal frame. His face seemed to have collapsed into the hollows beneath his prominent cheekbones, and every inch of his skin was etched with deep wrinkles, like a map of his suffering. The insides of his once-white pyjamas hung loose around his legs, fluttering far from his shrunken frame, while the frayed hems barely brushed his ankles.

It wasn't that his brothers or sons couldn't afford to buy him a new pair of pyjamas. Rather, such things no longer held any significance for Pholey Deehang. Life's little comforts had lost their meaning.

Instead, he wandered aimlessly, trudging down hills, crossing meadows, walking through bustling markets, silent woods, and desolate burial grounds. Clad in nothing but an old, threadbare shirt, he leaned on a stick for support, braving the cold winds that pierced his fragile bones. Occasionally, he was seen with a shawl carelessly slung over his back, but such comforts mattered little.

For Pholey Deehang, neither the chill of winter nor the warmth of summer's sun stirred his senses. Only the rains touched him—only the rains evoked fear.

Yet, no matter where his wandering steps took him, they unfailingly led him to the Bathou temple of Fhuwanji. There, he would roll the frayed hem of his yellowed pyjamas up to his knees and wade through the ankle-deep water that lingered in the temple courtyard, a relic of the great floods. He would settle on the driftwood near the shivling, sometimes speaking in murmurs to Baulungbwrai, the air around him heavy with unspoken sorrow.

Weeds and creeping vines had claimed the empty joukhoorei, twisting around its form, yet it hung in place, untouched since that fateful night. Pholey Deehang often gazed at it, as if expecting answers. When his eyes shifted to the horizon, all he saw was the vast expanse of Dwisikhlaa, its waters erasing all trace of Fhuwanji.

And sometimes, faint voices reached his ears—Girim Umata, Neishri, Keihoong, Pali, Gabkho. Voices that felt achingly familiar, heartbreakingly dear. Yet he could not place them. He could not name them.

That day, too, he sat by the shivling, staring blankly at the waters that surrounded him. Time dissolved. He did not know how long he remained there, nor did he notice when dusk fell. Pholey Deehang no longer noticed much of anything.

Dusk brought no flickering lamps to light his way, only the gentle ripple of Dwisikhlaa's waters flowing past—unapologetic, relentless. Above, a full moon ascended, bathing the world in silvery light. The same moon shone over the distant Umata farms and reflected upon the restless waters of the Dwisikhlaa.

Maya. Illusion.

As Pholey Deehang continued to sit and watch, sounds of fish surfacing on the waters of the Dwisikhlaa and the occasional night bird flying low to catch it punctuated the stillness of the evening. Then with one gentle but noticeable splash, a vision appeared in the waters. The same vision they had all seen on that fateful night of the great floods. Mertle. But this evening she didn't appear just as a lightning flash. This evening, she appeared, dived back into the waters and reappeared and dived in yet again. Pholey Deehang kept staring at the surface of the waters, hoping, without really realizing, for her to appear again.

And she did. Mertle emerged, revealing herself in her full, breath-taking glory. Dazzling, iridescent scales adorned her graceful, lithe body. Her head, almost human in shape, radiated an otherworldly charm, framed by long, flowing barbels that sprouted not from her mouth but from her head, like delicate strands of hair. Her tail, slender and elegantly forked, moved with a fluid grace, mesmerizing to behold.

As she turned, the sturdy, deep bronze shell on her back came into view, its surface unevenly patterned like the contours of ancient armour forged by nature itself. The shell exuded a quiet strength, complementing the ethereal gentleness that defined her presence.

Mertle embodied a perfect balance of grace and power—a being of profound beauty and quiet resilience.

A flood of moonbeams cascaded down, bathing the shell on Mertle's back in silver light. The beams refracted as they touched her bronze shell, sending their glow across the surface and illuminating the shivling below. What had once been a plain, uneven stone surface now appeared alive with strange inscriptions, brought into sharp relief by the interplay of light and shadow.

It was an inscription, without a doubt—but one that Pholey Deehang couldn't understand. He squinted, trying to read the symbols, but they remained cryptic, a riddle his mind couldn't solve.

Mertle splashed once more, sending droplets of water sparkling into the air. Each droplet shimmered like flecks of moonlit crystal, catching the light as they drifted towards Pholey Deehang. Gently, they settled on his heart and the white strands of hair on his head, each drop a soft whisper of light and memory.

'Glodew!' Mertle whispered.

Only Pholey Deehang heard.

The inscriptions on the shivling suddenly became more distinct. They began to make sense, like Pholey Deehang would understand them if he looked long and hard. He also sensed a strong, strange urge to place a hand on the letters on the stone shivling and to feel them, just like running a hand on braille. To know through the hand what the eyes could not tell. A little out of fear, a little out of reverence, Pholey Deehang surrendered to his urge and slowly stood up, walked close to the shivling and slowly ran a palm over the inscriptions on the stone structure. More glodew wafted in from the waters and tenderly alighted on the hand that was now cautiously moving all over the inscriptions. He looked at his hand. It was glittering with the glodew covering it like a child's hand while making sandcastles. As the glodew sat on the hand, Pholey Deehang started to hear soft voices inside him, in his heart and in his head. Voices which read the inscriptions to him in a way that he understood.

Awake! Look with your mind's eye. Search north and east. The Soul of the Joukhoorei is not lost forever. It has only lost its way.

'Baulungbwrai?' Pholey Deehang looked up. There was no one.

Beings from the Jataka are reincarnated only to take care of the Soul of the Joukhoorei. From every full moon to the next, the Jataka Creatures come one step closer to salvation. And on the night of the full moon of the month of Vaisakha, they shall leave the land of the mortals. Look for the Soul before they leave. Look along the Dwisikhlaa.

Look east. Look north.

Look towards where a hundred suns rise at dawn,

…and a thousand moons rise at night,

…and a million stars shine not in the Heavens but on the ground upon which the sage walks. Awake and look for it.

Pholey Deehang sat dazed and still, not knowing what to do. True, he had hopelessly been looking for Baulungbwrai. And if what the voice told him was true, and if he ever looked for and found the lost soul of the joukhoorei, maybe Baulungbwrai too would be found. Maybe the lost soul, if found, would lead to Baulungbwrai.

Aah! Hope! How it leads a person on!

The inscriptions on the shivling, however, didn't tell Pholey Deehang through the touch of the glodew whether he should bring the soul back to Fhuwanji, to Bathou. It just told him where to look for the soul. When the glodew lifted from him as gently as they had alighted and drifted back to Mertle, Pholey Deehang felt like he awoke from a deep slumber.

'Glodew!' she whispered once again, before disappearing into the waters. And once again, it was only Pholey Deehang who heard it. He stood and stared at the concentric circles on the surface of the Dwisikhlaa which Mertle caused. Circles, which were born when she dived in, and grew bigger and wider like a female with child, before dying at the birth of a new circle at the centre. Pholey Deehang saw birth, death and rebirth of the circle in the waters of the Dwisikhlaa, while the elemental soul of the circle, the water, remained the same throughout. Only now did Pholey Deehang understand what the rise and fall on the stone shivling was. Guiding inscriptions. But he wasn't aware that when the glodew swam back from him to merge with Mertle, they carried the message of the shivling to her as well.

Pholey Deehang wondered if the soul that Bathou mentioned was called Baulungbwrai. He wanted to know if Fhuwanji would be restored if Baulungbwrai was found and brought back. He wanted to know if Dwisikhlaa would go back to her original path, letting the fields, the grazing grounds and the homesteads of Fhuwanji that now lay in her womb resurface. But more than ever, he wanted to know where and how more than one sun could rise by day and more than one moon could rise by night. He wanted to know so many things before he went on his mission to look for the lost soul of the joukhoorei.

So, he returned the next night again to Bathou's home and sat on the drift root, staring at the waters, waiting for Mertle to appear. Even otherwise, no other purpose was left of Pholey Deehang's life. Even though he survived the floods, his heart and mind had sunk into the Dwisikhlaa that night. He no longer recognized anyone but Bathou. He no longer looked forward to anything but Baulungbwrai. Now, though, he looked forward to Mertle and waited for her to appear once more.

But that night she didn't appear.

He walked over to the shivling and ran his palm over its ruggedness but heard no voices because there was no glodew either, for that night wasn't one with a full moon. Pholey Deehang kept returning to the dilapidated temple on many more nights thereafter, in the hope of seeing Mertle. But she never once showed up. It was instead the Umata farm that became the centre of all activity in those subsequent nights.

The next full moon too was approaching fast, so Pholey Deehang decided not to wait any longer for Mertle to appear again with more guidance. Instead, he slung a cloth bag on one shoulder and on the other, his shawl. In the bag, he carried his prayer beads, some roasted rice powder, a few pieces of smoked and salted pork fat with a few shreds of sun-dried ginger. There was also some salt wrapped in a leaf and a copper bowl. With these, he set out east in search of the lost soul of the joukhoorei along the Dwisikhlaa, to reach on time, wherever Bathou wanted him to. Sometimes a farmer or a villager going that way gave him a ride on his cart. But most of the times he walked through the forested hills, watching out for signs that would lead him to the soul.

Whenever his feet ached and his breath got short, he sat by the shade of some tree or on a sunny rock by some stream. He then removed his thick boots of yak leather and sheep wool, stretched out his legs and aired his feet. If he felt like eating, he took out some rice powder in the bowl and ate it with the meat and some ginger. Sometimes he stopped by at villages where people gave him food and a place to rest for the night.

Unknown to him, Mertle was following him along the Dwisikhlaa.

Up on the mountains in the east, the month of Vaisakha had set in, and the snow was starting to melt and feed the many tiny brooks. Soon the brooks would widen, and many would flow down to join the Dwisikhlaa, though only later during the summer. And one of these streams, the Dwisanchi, would flow down across the Umata farm. But now, it was not the stream that Pholey Deehang paid attention to. It was the moon he looked out for, through the clouds and the pockets of thick foliage above him. When Mertle had appeared to Pholey Deehang and the glodew alighted on him, the voice had told him that if the lost soul of the joukhoorei was to be found, it had to be on the night of the full moon of Vaisakha, or never.

And the Vaisakha full moon was not too many nights away. He knew he didn't have much time. But how was he to go on, without knowing where to go or what signs to follow? How much ever he looked out for signs, the universe didn't let Pholey Deehang into any of its mysteries. Yet, he didn't give up and went on in his search. He went through villages, fields, forests and mountains, sometimes walking along the banks of the Dwisikhlaa. But sometimes, the river meandered away among the rocks and disappeared. He then had to follow the sound of the water, as he kept walking along the narrow foot-track. But he kept walking along the river. With hope and faith that he would find the lost soul of the joukhoorei, and Baulungbwrai, and that Fhuwanji would be reborn. There had also been times when despair sank all his hopes and he lay on the cold, hard ground and sobbed.

Then early one morning a few days into his journey, he awoke under the awnings of a small wayside shop at a village, but he couldn't open his eyes. He was blinded by a light too bright to be that of the rising sun, a light which came from the east. Still lying on his back, he rubbed his eyes and blinked. Slowly, after getting accustomed to the dazzle, he shielded his eyes with his hand and looked towards the light. He sat up and looked at what he thought was the sun, but he saw that there wasn't just one.

...a hundred suns rise at dawn...

Pholey Deehang's old heart at once knew that it was one of the signs, that it beckoned him to the soul of the joukhoorei. And he was shown the sign just where Dwisikhlaa was joined by a mountain brook. Villagers around there called this the Dwisanchi stream. The sign, he knew by instinct, told him to divert here and follow the Dwisanchi upstream from there on, towards the vision of the hundred suns. Towards north. Mertle followed him up the Dwisanchi. Hamlets got fewer and far between. Farther up, there were only a few scattered huts. Under his feet, the crackle of needles and cones of mountain trees too became lesser. The forest got scantier as the hills got quieter, except for the stray calls of insects or a bird on the cliffs. But he hadn't noticed any of these.

Instead, Pholey Deehang saw that there were more of pilgrims and monks along the track. Some were alone, some in groups; most on foot but some old and infirm were on yaks and horses. They all followed the narrow mountain path along the stream. They all seemed to go towards where '*a hundred suns rise at dawn*'. Pholey Deehang's waning faith began to resurface and that whole day he travelled towards those mythical hundred suns, without once stopping to rest. A pilgrim gave him a ride on his yak for some distance.

By dusk, all the hundred suns disappeared, and a spray of crimson painted the sky. The crimson turned to purple, then slowly to navy blue. Night was on its way. The mountains woke up to sounds of insects and night birds. But he was not scared. The gurgling sound of the Dwisanchi reassured him, making him feel safe, calm, and hopeful.

At nightfall, Pholey Deehang saw that '*a thousand moons*' rose from the same direction where a hundred suns had risen at dawn. He wanted to believe that he had found the place Bathou spoke to him about. At the same time, he was confused. 'Could a hundred suns and a thousand moons even be real at all? It was impossible!' he thought. He halted for the night beside a small group of monks. The monks spread mats on the ground and while some lay down, a few sat and took out their prayer beads. One of them shifted and made space on his mat for Pholey Deehang to lie down.

As the night grew darker and the mountain air grew colder, 'a million stars' began to glow well below the line where the skies met the earth. 'The stars are shining upon the ground!' Pholey Deehang was wonderstruck. Just like the voice that was brought on by the glodew had told him. All of a sudden, a shiver ran down his spine when he realized that all along, it was sages that he was walking with. Only, till now he saw them as Buddhist monks. He couldn't hold his excitement.

'Brother,' he asked the monk who shared his mat with him, 'what place is it up there with all those flickering lights?'

The monk smiled. 'The Dendup Gompa,' he replied.

'You are all headed that way?' Pholey Deehang asked him.

'Yes. We need to be there on time for the Vesak Poya observance. I suppose you call it Buddha Purnima,' the monk said, looking up at the sky.

Buddha Purnima! Full moon in the month of Vaisakha! Even though he didn't want to, the obvious spurted out of Pholey Deehang.

'Are you too, brother, in search of the lost soul of the joukhoorei?'

The monk shook his shaven head.

'No, ours is to pray for the emancipation of all souls in agony. To pray for the hundreds of souls trapped in the cycle of rebirth. Ours is not for the search of one lost soul.'

Pholey Deehang almost sighed in relief.

'And what about those hundred suns by dawn?' he asked, feeling more confident.

'One sun reflecting on the many rounded and curved surfaces of the Dendup Gompa's golden steeple.'

'And the thousand moons by night?'

'Light of the moon reflecting on the chortens around the gompa.'

'And the millions of stars on the ground?'

'Yak butter lamps around the chortens in the gompa.'

Pholey Deehang could no longer sit still. Yes, it was this place that he was to reach! From beyond the still and dark silhouettes of the tall, graceful trees, he heard the Dwisanchi rushing downhill. The darkness of the night never frightened her, nor did the light of day blind her. She was almost divine, he thought, almost a part of this mystical design of Bathou. What he didn't realize was that it was Mertle's presence in the waters that lent the enchantment to Dwisanchi during those hours before Vesak Poya.

'What is so special about Buddha Purnima in the Dendup Gompa?' Pholey Deehang asked, almost sure of having found his destination.

The monk proceeded to tell Pholey Deehang the legend of the man in whose memory the Dendup Gompa was built.

'Centuries ago,' the monk started his narration, 'an old woodcutter named Karma Dendup had as pets a dog, a squirrel and a rooster. One afternoon as he returned from the forest with a load of firewood, he saw that the rooster was pecking at a spider in an attempt to eat it. He shooed off the rooster and gently picked up the spider and nursed it back to good health. Soon the spider came to be accepted by the rest of the pets as one of them. Every morning, the dog would follow the woodcutter into the forest, be on the lookout for wild animals while his master fell trees and cut them into smaller pieces. In the afternoon, he followed the woodcutter back home. Karma Dendup would then sell the firewood and bring back food for all of them.'

Pholey Deehang listened with rapt attention. Everything that night was turning out to be so enthralling! The monk went on.

'So, while Karma Dendup and the dog were gone, the rooster pecked at and dug up the few vegetables its master tried to cultivate. The squirrel bit into the dried corn saved up for the chill winter months and left them unfit to eat. The spider too wove webs that hung all over the little cottage, causing painful itches to Karma Dendup.

'Yet he continued to feed and shelter all of them. Gradually, Karma Dendup grew older and older and then a time came when he could no longer venture out into the forest to cut wood. The rashes on his skin got worse and they caused fever and breathlessness in him. Soon, food started getting scarce for all five beings. When the last morsels were exhausted, the squirrel, the rooster and the spider abandoned the old, sick and starving Karma Dendup and left in search of another master. They asked the dog if he would like to accompany them. But the dog refused. He instead sat by his master's bedside, not leaving there even to go and look out for food for itself. Legend says,' the monk went on, 'that both Karma Dendup and his dog starved until their souls flew out of their mortal bodies at the same instance.

'Legend also says,' the monk continued, 'that the dog was in fact the Buddha, in one of his earlier incarnations.'

Pholey Deehang gasped.

'And the cottage where Karma Dendup lived and died with his dog came to be revered as the Dendup Gompa by the villagers. Karma Dendup's soul attained emancipation, but it still chose to remain and watch over the Buddha, never to abandon him. Just as the Buddha, in his incarnation as a dog in the Jataka legend, never abandoned Karma Dendup the woodcutter. And so even today, Karma Dendup stands in the form of the Tree of Emancipation, watching over the Buddha in the gompa up there.'

The monk pointed towards the higher reaches of the mountain, towards Dendup Gompa, before resuming his tale.

'Estranged souls come to this tree because the compassion of Karma Dendup purifies and helps them to attain their emancipation, provided they have served the purpose of their birth.'

'And the squirrel, the rooster and the spider?' Pholey Deehang asked in complete awe.

'They, older monks say, have gone through many more births but are yet to be liberated from the cycle of rebirth,' the monk explained.

After he heard the whole narration, the words *Jataka legend* kept ringing in Pholey Deehang's mind.

'*…beings from the Jataka are reborn only to take care of it…*'

Pholey Deehang walked the rest of the path in his search for the lost soul of the joukhoorei in the company of the monks.

9

The Hundredth Jerutu Escapes!

The oowii-oowiis had meanwhile reached the Umata farm from Dendup Gompa. Sunny and Sandie perched atop a tree from where they could see the Umata house as they waited for Dunu to return from school in the valley below. A little distance away from the tree, Kelman was burning a pile of fallen leaves that he had raked in. And inside the house, Hazel incessantly chattered on and paced about, doing every little chore without which existence itself would be doubtful.

'Blessed Buddha! How much mess can one little girl make!' she said, first to herself and then to all the books and colouring pencils that lay strewn about on Dunu's bed. 'Couldn't you walk back to your own places, eh?' she told the pencils and laughed at her own joke.

She moved around the room picking socks from the floor, pyjamas from the arms of a chair, pulling out toffee wrappers from the pen stand, dusting off pencil shavings from the study table and clearing the whole place. Then she pulled the curtains on the windows to filter the strong afternoon sun. 'Clear up, clear up! Only so that my little girl comes back from school and messes up all over again,' she told herself.

Just then she heard a noise in the bottom drawer of Dunu's study table. The only one with the latch.

'Mousie? I kind of knew it! I just knew it!' she said, dropping back on the floor whatever she had picked from it till now with great effort. 'There has to be a mouse in here with all that mess, shouldn't it? O come off now!' she yelled at the shoe on her left foot as she tugged at it with her right hand. 'Hurry now, mousie won't wait for you!'

Then with as much stealth as her ample body could muster, Hazel crouched on her knees and slowly proceeded towards the drawer. Clutching the shoe, her right hand was raised and ready to bring the shoe down upon the noisy mouse the moment the left hand would open the latch of the drawer. But when she flung open the door, half out of terror and half out of challenge, expecting utter chaos first inside the drawer and then outside it, she was completely taken aback to find that there was nothing there other than peace.

And a green coconut. No mouse.

Hazel plonked upon the wooden floor with a sigh of relief, facing the open drawer and looking at the coconut though not really seeing it. All she saw was that there was no mouse in there.

'It fled, you scared it!' she was telling her shoe with a guffaw as she pushed it back onto her foot.

It was only when she looked again into the drawer after that brief distraction with the shoe that she saw the coconut.

'Oh? A coconut? Now what's a green coconut doing in the drawer here?' She brought it out, holding it in her hands to inspect it. The coconut was lying on its side on a small towel. There was a small tear on the leaf that covered the top, where there was a hole.

'Okay, so you were the mouse! Nut-ty mouse you are, aren't you? But wait! Aren't you too big for a coconut?' She paused. She turned the nut in her hands, her gaze sharpening as she studied it intently. For a moment, she was still, her eyes locked on the small, unassuming object. And then, as if a thunderbolt had struck her, she screamed.

'IT'S THE COCONUT OF THE BEINGS OF THE DARK!'

And she ran out with the speed of a typhoon, with the coconut held as far away from herself as she could in her outstretched hands. She ran straight to where Kelman was turning the leaves in the fire with a long stick and hurled the coconut right into the fire there.

'Oh, dear me! Oh!' She panted, more out of fright than for her sprint.

When the large coconut hit the fire with a thunderous crash, a shower of splinters erupted, sending shards flying. Sunny's attention was immediately drawn to the spectacle. Bewildered, his orange-thatched head perked up once again, standing tall as if reaching towards the heavens.

'Sandie look!' Sunny screamed. 'The coconut! Hazel just flung it into the fire!' With that, he dropped down from the tree, Sandie perched on his back, and landed on Kelman's shoulder, ready to distract him. As always in such moments, the oowii-oowiis fell into an unspoken, perfectly synchronized action, their movements as fluid and instinctive as ever.

A startled Kelman dropped the stick with which he was turning the leaves. While Sunny ran to the stick, Sandie stayed behind to crawl about Kelman's nape. Then she ventured up his ears, even poking a limb to tickle the insides. Finally, she wiggled her way under his shirt down his back. She tickled him all over and while Kelman did some energetic, yet unknown dance steps, Sunny and Ronie pushed one end of the stick into the fire to reach the coconut. When the stick touched the nut, they pushed harder and harder, this way and that, till they succeeded in rolling the coconut out of the fire on the other side. Sandie now took the risk of getting slapped and squashed, yet she stuck all ten limbs around Kelman's round face and sat her two fistfuls of a body *spat* upon the boy's face. So, the poor boy could neither see what was going on nor scream in alarm. And while she kept the boy, Ronie and Sunny rolled the coconut away from there. When they were done, Sandie planted a resounding kiss on Kelman's cheek, dropped herself to the ground and ran towards Sunny and Ronie.

The thin, usually absent-minded Kelman felt his cheek, rubbed his eyes, and looked for the stick. It was still there. He looked up at the tree. There were a couple of squirrels there, just plain brown ones. He raised his stick and shooed them away, before quietly going back to turning the leaves. The smoke from the fire carried the lazy, delicious smell of burned, dry leaves all over the Umata farm.

Far away from the fire, by the stream, the oowii-oowiis were stunned as they stared at the coconut in horror. The leaf cover of the coconut was partly burned, and the coconut was empty.

The hundredth Jerutu had escaped!

'Holy smoke!' Sandie sighed.

'Shit! Shit!' Ronie clenched his claws and struck the coconut.

'But it won't be able to go far, Ronie, remember what Old Monk said, about Jerutus deriving their energy only from fluid? If it's on dry land, it won't have enough energy to whoosh around. Moreover, it can't even fly long distances!' Sunny talked sense this time.

'But boys, that there in the stream, them be waters. Them not be a-fluid?' Sandie too talked some sense this time.

Sunny suddenly looked towards the fire. 'Could he have fallen into the fire and burned out?'

'Eh, Sunny! Smoke be born from them fires, boy, and not be a-dying in one,' Sandie snubbed him.

'So, what now?' Sunny asked.

'Dunu!' replied Ronie.

'Dunu?' Sandie repeated.

'Yes, Dunu,' Ronie asserted.

And the oowii-oowiis went as close to the house as was safe for them and stationed themselves in a way from where they could see the entrances to the house which Dunu normally used. They also took care so that they themselves were not seen.

Back inside the house, Hazel had raised a verbal thunderstorm. Dunu had arrived from school and Hazel wanted to know, and know right away, what the coconut was doing inside her drawer. 'Did you even know or didn't you that the whole green nut sat there inside your drawer, Dunu? And what a puny effort to cover itself under that equally puny leaf. Bah!' Hazel confronted Dunu.

Dunu was taken aback. Guilt clamped her stomach like the clips on Hazel's laundry line, for she was caught keeping things from Hazel and Grandpa. Her eyes welled up. This was the first time in her little life that she had kept something from them. At the same time, she had to keep her commitment towards the oowii-oowiis too. But most importantly, she had to protect the coconut and the soul in it.

She tried to explain, 'Hazel, look...'

'I looked! And thank my Buddha I looked! Or else I wouldn't have seen that devil's vessel and the devil would then come out of that drawer to first sit on your study desk, then on your chair, then on your head and then on all our heads to vacuum out our brains and take our hearts and souls...'

'HAZEL!' Dunu screamed as she stomped her foot and let the scream linger on for many minutes. That was the only way to stop Hazel from rambling on and on. Meanwhile, she hurried to the drawer where she had kept the coconut and found it unlatched and opened, and the coconut missing.

'WHAT DID YOU DO WITH THE NUT? And the soul in it ... WHAT DID YOU DO TO IT?'

For once Dunu was more tensed and petrified about something other than Hazel's fury. She was anxious about the escaped Jerutu.

'Blessed Buddha! My Buddha! Now did you just say there was a soul in there? In that nut? In this house? No wonder there were strange noises coming out from the drawer! I knew it! I just knew it! How could anyone even think that anything around here could escape my notice, eh? Oh, my Buddha!' Hazel started to rant once again.

'Hazel, stop! And please, Hazel, what did you do to the soul? I need to find it. It needs help, Hazel, our help...' Dunu was crying loudly now.

'Oh? And since when did mysterious souls start seeking the help of little girls who are themselves helpless?' Hazel argued, not one to let go easily.

'This is a harmless soul, Hazel,' Dunu tried to make her understand the gravity of the situation, 'now stop arguing and tell me, please, what did you do to it? O please, Hazel!'

'My dear little girl, I found no soul,' Hazel said, calming down a bit.

If Hazel said she found no soul, Dunu knew it had to be so. Because Hazel was as thickly unpretentious and honest as a mattress.

'But the matter has to go to Grandpa!' Hazel insisted.

And so, she pulled Dunu by the hand and led her to Grandpa, continuously talking to Dunu, to herself and once even to the soul which she hadn't seen.

Grandpa was outside, supervising Minkai's task of cleaning the long rows of fowl coops. The moment Hazel stepped out of the house and marched towards Grandpa pulling Dunu after her, the oowii-oowiis followed them, though at a safe distance.

'Now, Grandpa, look here,' Hazel began with the air of immense authority, 'we have a bigger mess in there where we live than the mess in these foul-smelling houses where these fowls live!'

Grandpa turned around to look at Hazel's parade.

'Minkai, my boy,' he said, adjusting his wide-brimmed hat, 'now get ready for some ballistic babble-o-blah!' And the two laughed as Hazel's voice approached.

'Do you even know, Grandpa, that our little girl had been harbouring a soul right there in her study desk?' Hazel said without waiting for breath.

The oowii-oowiis stepped closer.

'But it has escaped, Grandpa, I'll tell you everything,' Dunu said apologetically, 'but before all else, I need to find it. The soul … it isn't mine.'

'Oh? I sure can see it isn't yours.' The inner ends of Hazel's eyebrows came low and close to each other and the outer ends shot up. 'You're hale and alive.'

'No … I mean … it doesn't belong to me, I was merely a custodian. I was asked to just take care of it.'

'By?' Hazel fumed.

'By…' Dunu fumbled with an answer when a movement behind the coop caught her attention.

It was Ronie. He had moved close to the coop just to make himself be seen by Dunu. He shook his head with the weather cock on it, gesturing her not to tell them about the oowii-oowiis. So now Dunu suddenly looked at Hazel with soulful eyes and clasped her stomach with the free hand.

'I haven't had anything to eat since I got back from school, Hazel, and on top of that you've been…' her voice almost broke, '…reprimanding me and…'

Now the outer ends of Hazel's eyebrows fell, and the inner ends shot up.

'Oh, oh! I … how could I! Mercy me! Oh my…' She left Dunu holding on to Grandpa and hurried away towards her kitchen, unable to forgive herself for her thoughtlessness.

'But, Grandpa, also please see into this souled matter,' she babbled away as she hurried towards the kitchen, 'this is no joke to let off with a wave of your hand and … you!' she said, suddenly looking down at a snail on her path, 'move off!' She stepped aside to save it. 'I'll be back in a moment with the milk and some freshly baked raspberry cake.' Her

voice was going softer and farther but it yet went on, '...
but I am not going to give up on that hot air! Grandpa, you
shouldn't either!'

'Ho! I am not to give up on the hot air!' Grandpa laughed.
'That means I am to pass them more often!' He guffawed.
Minkai too doubled over with laughter.

But Dunu didn't. Grandpa noticed it and saw that this
time it wasn't just a matter of letting a lizard lose in Hazel's
room. Dunu was genuinely tensed and not at all hungry.

'I just need to find it, Grandpa,' she said, and started
sobbing.

'Okay, okay, now tell me, what is this soul Hazel was
making a hue and cry about? It's not a soul really, is it?'
Grandpa asked her.

'It is, Grandpa, I'm sorry I should've told you, but it is.'

'Did Hazel see it? Has it been haunting people around?'
Now even Grandpa looked nervous.

'The soul?' Dunu asked Grandpa but replied before he
said anything. 'No, Hazel didn't know about it till I blurted
out a moment ago. Because she threw away the coconut in
which the soul was put.' She looked up at Grandpa with
sudden recollection and asked, 'You remember the coconut?
That night of the fire near the coconut palms?'

'Oh yes, yes! Whatever with that coconut?'

So Dunu went on to tell Grandpa about the oowii-oowiis,
about the soul in the nut and about Owl. She also told him
about how the soul came to be in her drawer. 'The oowii-
oowiis had to go to Dendup Gompa, Grandpa, to meet Old
Monk. He alone knows about such souls,' she related what
was told to her, 'and because the vulnerable soul could not
be left unattended, they trusted me to safe keep it till they

returned.' Her eyes filled up when she said, 'I have failed them, Grandpa, I have failed their trust. They said I was their friend, but I let them down.' Her voice broke into a sob. After many years, Grandpa once again felt the strain of fear and uncertainty weighing down upon his old heart.

'The oowii-oowiis are back from the gompa, Grandpa, I saw Ronie the rooster over there just moments ago. I need to meet them. They're actually nice and fun, and the least evil and scary as Hazel supposes. Rather, it is they who are scared of Hazel.'

Grandpa led Dunu to the felled log beside the coop and they both sat down on it.

'Ah well, do you think I may meet up with the hola-holas?' Grandpa offered to help.

'The oowii-oowiis!' Dunu corrected him.

'Yes, them? Maybe together we can help find the soul and send it back to where it belongs?' He tried to pacify her.

Dunu's face lit up at once and she wiped the tears off her eyes with her sleeve. 'Golly gimplink! You're such a darling, Grandpa,' she said, standing up on the log to plant a kiss on the old man's arctic circle.

'Now?' she asked him.

'Now.' Grandpa nodded.

'Here?' Dunu asked.

'Mmm, no, not here,' he said after a moment's thought. 'Hazel may come up any moment and disintegrate our little union. Her hullabaloo will affect our search for the soul, right?'

'Right! Right!' she agreed. Dunu felt so relieved. It actually helped to have an understanding grown-up to confide in, she realized.

So, they left Minkai at the coop and walked slowly away towards the long row of oaks, as if they were just taking a stroll. They pretended that nothing serious had happened. Dunu gestured the oowii-oowiis to follow them. When they at last met, Grandpa veiled his amusement upon seeing the strange creatures.

'Hello, beautiful creations of the Lord!' he said, successfully camouflaging his bewilderment.

'Grandpa?' All three greeted in a chorus.

'Yeah … Grandpa.' Dunu nodded.

'Yeah … Grandpa!' Grandpa looked at Dunu and agreed with her.

'I … uh … the soul … it escaped.' Dunu felt like crying.

'We know,' Sunny spoke for all three.

'You know?' Dunu asked surprised.

'We saw Hazel hurling the nut into the fire,' Sunny told them.

'We saved the nut, but the soul wasn't there,' Ronie added.

'The Jerutu be escape!' Sandie quipped.

There was a moment's silence.

'But will someone now please tell me about this soul in the coconut?' Grandpa asked.

Dunu looked at the oowii-oowiis. And so, the oowii-oowiis went ahead and told Grandpa about the soul in the coconut. They also told him about Old Monk in the gompa and all that he had told them about the Tree of Emancipation. And about Jerutu. That it is the hundredth and the last Jerutu. And how Old Monk referred to the oowii-oowiis as beings from the Jataka.

'And Old Monk also said that for about a decade now, Jerutu is unconsciously looking for, and moving towards, someone or something with whom it shared a bond of many, many years,' Sunny added.

'And that this smoky Jerutu be living l-o-n-g near a-Shiva. Old Monk be calling Shiva not as Shiva, Grandpa, he be calling him Ba-thou,' Sandie elaborated.

Grandpa suddenly looked up. In the depths of his mind, the word *Bathou*, and that Jerutu lived long near Bathou, unleashed a chain of memories which he had long left to slumber. For whenever he thought of those times, loss and yearning stabbed his heart and slaughtered him from inside. Girim Umata no longer had the courage to face such pain. But now those memories were being knocked at.

'Do you happen to know Old Monk by any other name?' he eagerly asked the oowii-oowiis.

The oowii-oowiis looked at one another and then shook their heads.

'Did Old Monk say Bathou?' Grandpa asked them, but actually to only convince himself. Because no-one in those parts of the mountains said Bathou. They said Shiva. And Kailashnath. And Omkar. But not Bathou.

'Did Old Monk also say a decade? That's ten years. Dunu's age. The time since the great floods at…' He paused. A faraway look came upon his eyes. A look of going back into time only to suffer inexpressible pain and loss all over again, to overcome which he had given everything. Dunu never saw such a look in his eyes before.

'Grandpa?' She reached out for his hand. He sought it and held it in a way as if without holding on to that little hand, he would collapse.

'Are you okay, Grandpa?' she asked.

'Why, of course! Mmm, yes, yes! I was just wondering how we can trace the hundredth Jerutu,' he said, veiling the rising restlessness inside him. What he didn't say was that a few questions were beginning to rise in his mind.

Could the lost soul be that of Baulungbwrai? If it is not, could Baulungbwrai be somewhere around these snow-capped mountains, around Mount Swrang? In the high Himalayas, closer to Bathou? Is it towards him that the Jerutu is instinctively moving?

10

Pholey Deehang Meets Old Monk

It was morning when Pholey Deehang arrived at the Dendup Gompa. Elaborate preparations were afoot there for the Vesak Poya celebration. It had been long since Pholey Deehang saw such festivity and so many people at the same time, at the same place. It made him nervous, he felt lost. Newly put-up prayer flags fluttered from horizontal strings strung from one chorten to another and from long, vertical poles of freshly cut bamboo.

The morning sun gently kissed the flags, casting a warm glow before reflecting off the stupas and chortens, each freshly painted and polished to a brilliant sparkle. Every piece of copper in the gompa gleamed as if it were a mirror, catching the light in a dance of reflection. Lanterns, crafted from mountain grass, cloth, and paper, were hung from the gate all the way to the main doorway of the monastery. By dusk, they would all come alive with light.

Monks were everywhere—sages, as Pholey Deehang now saw them. Some were so small, perhaps still with milk teeth yet to fall, while others were so old that their memories had blurred, unable to recall events tied to the years of their birth, and thus unable to reckon their age. After the Vesak Poya rituals, some of these monks would embark on a three-month summer retreat, delving deeper into meditation, learning, and penance.

There were also pilgrims—many of them—and villagers who had travelled from as far as the valleys of Bouzu and Lushi in Bhutan, and from the valley of Dobba, north of Kindoree. The villagers came to Dendup Gompa not for the rituals themselves, but to help with the arrangements, to cook for the pilgrims, and to assist visitors. It was believed that serving the monks and pilgrims during the auspicious hours of Vesak Poya near the Swrang Buddha brought as much blessing as meditating and chanting prayers at the Buddha's altar, striving to transform an impure being into a pure one.

There were those who arrived with offerings—milk, rice, raisins, and honey—to be cooked together in large vessels, to serve as sweetened rice for anyone present at the time of the offering. Others came simply to offer yak butter for the lamps, which would burn for forty-eight hours straight, illuminating the night of Vesak Poya and the night that followed.

Makeshift sheds were set up along the periphery of the monastery's grounds, providing space for cooking and places for visitors to rest. There were also shelters for ponies, yaks, and horses—the faithful companions of many pilgrims who had arrived by horseback. Scattered around the grounds were a few large clay pots with crackling log fires, offering warmth to those who had made the arduous trek up the mountain to the gompa. But the largest marquee stood around the Tree of Emancipation, its presence commanding attention. Large groups of people had already begun to sit there, to listen to the sermons of the senior monks and visiting teachers of the various sects of Buddhism. Most, however, arrived to listen to Old Monk. Yet some came just to look at the boughs of the blessed Tree and feel sanctified by just being under it. The whole ambience made Pholey Deehang somewhat dizzy. For he had now, since long, been habituated to looking out at and seeing only miles and miles of the tranquil waters of the Dwisikhlaa.

There was not a single movement within those watery miles, other than a bird swooping down to the waters to catch a fish or a stray boatman rowing his harvest to some market downstream. He had grown habituated to silence all around him. Silence, for there was no Baulungbwrai. Silence, for there was no Girim Umata, and silence, for there was simply no one else there any longer, for him to speak with and listen to.

For there was no village, and no huts with flickering lamps by dusk. He was left all alone. And now suddenly he was standing in the midst of hundreds of people and as suddenly, there were thousands of flickering lamps all around him. This sudden and sweeping difference made him forget what purpose brought him to this incredible place. He looked all around him in absolute wonder. Then his gaze moved beyond the festivity and out into the skies, towards the lofty peak of Mount Swrang. It was still clad with snow. And that snow, Pholey Deehang saw, was lying in the formation of a trident. Like the one in Bathou's temple in Fhuwanji.

'Bathou ... Ah, yes!' And Pholey Deehang instantly remembered his purpose of being at the gompa. It was his search for the lost soul of the joukhoorei that had brought him there. Bathou had told him that he would find it there. There, where *a hundred suns rise at dawn ... and a thousand moons rise at night ... and a million stars shine not in the Heavens but on the ground upon which the sage walks...*' But how could he look for a soul here in this multitude? Here where it was difficult to even look for a human? He looked around for someone whom he could ask. There were people to assist pilgrims and visitors, but he did not know if he could ask them about a lost soul. Would they mock him?

He realized he was losing courage; and hope as well. He soaked in the many sights and chants as he walked slowly along with the crowd, looking for a place to sit and stretch his tired limbs. He was heading towards one of the clay pots with fire when he saw little monks taking around small bowls of water and steaming herbal tea among the visitors and pilgrims. One such little monk came and stood near Pholey Deehang and offered him tea.

Pholey Deehang gratefully took the bowl and held it in his cupped hands. The warmth of the tea seeped through the bowl to reach his hands, rejuvenating and calming him. He took slow, long sips from the bowl and the tea now reached every part of his being to warm him from inside. His courage was slowly finding its way back. So was hope. After a few sips when Pholey Deehang looked up from the bowl, he saw an aged monk looking down at him and smiling. There was a glint in the monk's eyes, of a long wait having reached an end. The smile stretched his wrinkles. He sat down next to Pholey Deehang.

'So, you have arrived at last, Pholey Deehang, I waited long for you,' the monk said.

Pholey Deehang almost dropped the bowl of tea in surprise. The monk quickly stretched out his hand and held the bowl, as well as Pholey Deehang's hands.

'Tremble not. I am just a monk here.'

Pholey Deehang bowed his head low.

'You come as a bearer of Bathou's commands, don't you? Bathou of Fhuwanji?'

Pholey Deehang could only nod.

'You come for the lost soul of the joukhoorei, don't you?'

Pholey Deehang nodded once again. A cold breeze ruffled his shirt. Old Monk removed the shawl from Pholey Deehang's shoulders and wrapped him with it.

'I've heard of a great flood there. Does Fhuwanji remain?'

'In Dwisikhlaa's abyss, yes.' Pholey Deehang never believed that Fhuwanji remained no more. For him, Fhuwanji always existed. Wherever.

Old Monk continued asking questions one after the other. And Pholey Deehang went on answering them, though almost in a daze.

'Does Bathou's home there exist?'

'It does,' he now replied.

'In Dwisikhlaa's abyss?'

'No, in ankle-deep water.'

'And the stone shivling?'

'With water weed and creepers crawling over it, yes.'

Then there was a long pause. And during that pause Pholey Deehang suddenly ceased to hear all noise that was all along droning around him. Instead, he thought he began hearing the glodew and it was only that which he heard and nothing else. At that moment he even ceased to see any of the sights around him. Because he saw only the glodew.

'Could Mertle be around?' he wondered.

After a long while Old Monk spoke again. 'And the joukhoorei?'

Pholey Deehang stood up abruptly, stunned beyond measure at the mention of the joukhoorei.

'Who are you?' he asked Old Monk.

'They all call me Old Monk. And the joukhoorei?' he repeated.

'It hangs upon the shivling.'

'You have come for the lost soul of the joukhoorei?'

'Who are you?' Pholey Deehang asked a second time with increasing curiosity.

Old Monk only smiled this time before replying. 'You will find the hundredth Jerutu, the lost soul of the joukhoorei here tomorrow night, under the Tree of Emancipation. It will be the night of Vesak Poya, when the moon is at its roundest, and when its light is the brightest.'

'I come to take the lost soul of the joukhoorei, Old Monk, to where it belongs. To the joukhoorei in the Bathou temple at Fhuwanji.'

'What purpose will that serve?' Old Monk asked Pholey Deehang.

'What purpose will the soul serve otherwise?' Pholey Deehang responded.

Old Monk now pointed at the bollongs and the jaikhlongs on the Tree of Emancipation.

'My dear Pholey Deehang, you see those? Each of those ninety-nine bollongs has a Jerutu in it and each of those thousands of jaikhlongs has a soul in it. They are all waiting for their ultimate deliverance from the cycle of rebirth.'

'What does the lost soul of the joukhoorei have to do with that?' Pholey Deehang wished to know.

'It alone has everything to do with that,' Old Monk explained with profound calm. 'Without the lost soul of the joukhoorei, which is the hundredth Jerutu, the remaining ninety-nine Jerutus will not receive emancipation. These Jerutus have waited for nearly a century now. If the hundredth Jerutu is not here at the brightest hour on the night of the Vesak Poya, these souls will fall into immense trauma for all time to come, being able to neither return to the mortal nor merge with the cosmic immortal.'

'It does not matter to me,' Pholey Deehang replied, almost getting fretful that he would not be allowed to take the soul with him. 'I come to take the hundredth Jerutu and that alone matters to me.'

'The reason for that?'

'Revival of my Fhuwanji.'

'How?'

'If the soul is restored into the joukhoorei, Fhuwanji will be revived.'

'But the soul is a Jerutu. It survives only on fluid though it itself is air. So how do you hope to nurture the soul without fluid in the joukhoorei?'

'The joukhoorei can be filled with jou.'

'For whom to sip?'

'For Baulungb…'

Pholey Deehang suddenly looked up. He had never got used to the fact that Baulungbwrai was no more. A flash of recollection sped through his mind, of what the old folks had long ago said. *Fhuwanji exists only if Baulungbwrai does.*

'You have been assured of Fhuwanji's revival?' Old Monk asked Pholey Deehang.

'I have been assured of finding the lost soul of the joukhoorei,' he replied.

'By Bathou?'

'By Bathou.'

'Had Bathou asked you to take the soul back with you to Fhuwanji?'

Pholey Deehang did not respond. Because Bathou hadn't.

'My friend,' Old Monk said slowly, 'all who had been uprooted from your village and settled elsewhere and made themselves a part of their new dwellings, will now have neither the courage nor the will to unsettle all over again, only to start from scratch. They are yet to recover from the emotional and physical trauma of that displacement. Do you expect them to willingly come forward to go through the same trauma all over again with yet another relocation?'

Old Monk paused. 'Will you, for that matter?'

Pholey Deehang thought long before replying. 'I will.'

'What about your children and their spouses? And their children?'

Pholey Deehang could not answer for his children and their spouses. And for their children.

'Fhuwanji's natives, who have already survived the great flood, will yet continue to survive even without the Jerutu being taken back to the Bathou temple. They will not languish.' Old Monk looked up at the bollongs and the jaikhlongs. They looked splendid in the afternoon sunlight, almost divine as they caught the sun's rays, retained a part of it and reflected the rest. A couple of monks arrived to ask Old Monk to take his seat under the Tree of Emancipation. Visiting monks and disciples were waiting for him there. But Old Monk continued to make Pholey Deehang understand why the soul was needed at the gompa at that hour. 'But the ninety-nine Jerutus and the thousands of souls in those jaikhlongs will, Pholey Deehang, they will languish without the hundredth Jerutu. Consider, my friend, decide wisely and with compassion. But then...' He tapped Pholey Deehang lightly on the shoulder as he stood up to go, '...that which is destined to be, will yet be!' And Old Monk merged into the crowd that brimmed with robes of maroon and orange. Colours of the sun, colours of the ultimate radiance.

Pholey Deehang got up and slowly followed the crowd into the main altar to pay his obeisance to the Swrang Buddha. As he stood before the Swrang Buddha, he noticed the Buddha's closed eyes and the lotus position, the Padmaasanaa, in which the Buddha sat. He looked so much like Shiva. As the chants fell and rose all around Pholey Deehang, and as the smell of burning incense mixed with the fragrance of sandalwood, pine latex and eaglewood from the fire in the clay pots wafted among the people, he found himself closing his eyes and getting transported to the Bathou temple at Fhuwanji. Just outside, Dwisanchi let the water prayer wheels gyrate gently and a certain vision flashed there ahead of the full moon, because there was as much light in the gompa now, enhanced by prayer and meditation, as would be on a full-moon night.

Mertle.

The sun refracting from the gompa's stupa fell on her shell and every droplet of water that she splashed up caught a bit of this light and shone like tiny crystals of sun. Slowly, a very gentle spray of these soft, illuminated crystals swam towards Pholey Deehang and rested on his heart. The essence of the water prayer wheel, which these crystals carried with them, soothed Pholey Deehang's disturbed heart.

Just then he thought he heard that same, familiar whisper. 'Glodew!' he thought aloud.

He looked for Mertle but saw only the water prayer wheels. Yet the glodew were there, alighting on him. Despite the crowd, only Pholey Deehang saw the glodew.

'Look with your mind's eye. Search north and east. The Soul of the Joukhoorei is not lost forever. It has only lost its way…'

Pholey Deehang once again heard within him the message of the inscriptions on the stone shivling. He felt like it wasn't at the Gompa that he was standing but before the shivling in the Bathou temple at Fhuwanji.

'But why?' he wondered. He was confused and felt deceived. 'If I am not to take it with me, if the lost soul of the joukhoorei has a different purpose to serve, why did Bathou send me to look for it?'

He opened his eyes. The glodew were gone. 'Was it that I may lead the glodew and Mertle here? But what purpose may they serve in Bathou's designs for the lost soul of the joukhoorei?' Pholey Deehang ladled out a scoop of yak butter from a big pot, kept next to the rows of lamps, into one of the many copper lamps kept aside for devotees to light. He then lit the lamp and knelt down in front of the Buddha but when he prayed, he found himself praying to Bathou.

'Maybe,' he thought, 'if the joukhoorei is given back its soul, Baulungbwrai too will reappear. And then so will Fhuwanji.'

Now that the hour of finding the lost soul of the joukhoorei was near and now that he heard all that Old Monk had to say, confusion and despair rose in Pholey Deehang's heart and mind. A heart and a mind which were lingering on the verges of insanity for a decade since the great flood, suddenly found themselves being faced with having to make a sane choice. He was left in an emotional turmoil. Bathou's guidance too for him was only until here, and no further.

'So must I just give up the soul after finding it?' He couldn't decide. All he decided for the moment was to be there till the Vesak Poya moon rose to its highest and brightest.

11

Jerutu Is Still at Large

Hazel marched into the kitchen wondering whether all of it was a dream or a reality.

'How could Hazel let a stray soul come so close to her Dunu?' Hazel had a habit of speaking her thoughts, just as other people would think quietly in their minds. 'And then leave her hungry in the stomach? Merciful Buddha, make me atone. Oh! Show me mercy!'

When she walked into the kitchen, she saw Brum sitting on his hind legs, staring at the cupboard.

'Ah, you breathing sack of fur and fat! So, you have already sniffed out the cake there, have you, eh? Not that you get some now, boy. You already got a big slice when the cake was just out of the oven, you forgot that? And why wouldn't you? When you are only b-r-a-w-n-s...' and she swayed her generous middle in rhythm to the word brawn, to mock the equally ample dog, 'and no brains. Brains, as has good ole Hazel.'

But today Brum ignored Hazel. He just stared at the cupboard, alert and somewhat puzzled. There were small and big jars with cookies and spices inside the cupboard, as well as on top of it. There were pots of pickles and metal jars with smoked meat too, lined on shelves below the cups, bowls and saucers. It was arranged thus so that Dunu could reach for the snacks without help.

Brum sometimes came around to have a good sniff at freshly smoked meat but on those occasions, his face looked greedy and silly, with drool dotting the floor under his chin. That day, however, as he sat staring, his face looked neither greedy, nor silly. Rather, it looked surprised and confused.

'Brum oi!' Hazel tried to gently shove his big butt aside, as she kept talking to him. 'If you may please do me the favour of moving your tail.' Brum slid only his tail to one side. 'And the behind to which it is attached.' He stubbornly kept the behind just where it was. 'I can walk faster around here. And if I walk faster…'

Brum looked at her and exhaled noisily, showing much disdain at her constant jabbering, for it was distracting his focus from the thing he was so intently staring at.

'…I can work more efficiently. Unlike you! Hah! But I don't know why I still love you to pieces, ole boy!'

She gave a quick rub behind his ears and went about placing a saucepan on the fire to warm some milk for Dunu and opened the cupboard to take out the jar of milk. When she brought it out, Brum almost jumped to reach the jar. That was what he was staring at.

'Hey! Hey! Behave now, you fluff of a dog! But why? You never do that?' she reprimanded Brum as she opened the lid of the jar and poured the milk into the pan. 'Milk, anyway, isn't something you would drool over, boy, then why this show of athletics?' But even before the milk reached the pan, Hazel let out an enormous shriek and, dropping the milk all over herself and Brum, she ran out of the kitchen, screaming and flaying her arms.

'Smoke! No, hot gas! In cold milk! A face of smoke! Help!' She ran towards the coops where she had left Dunu and Grandpa. But they weren't there. That scared Hazel even more.

'Grandpa! Joyan! Someone help!'

'Jerutu! That must be Jerutu!' Sunny said, all excited and almost running out into the open. But Ronie jumped onto his tail to stop him.

'Ouch! And what was that for?' Sunny scowled at Ronie.

'To stop you from running out there and scaring Hazel,' Ronie scolded Sunny. 'She already frets and fumes over us and if she chances upon one of us now when she's in an absolute frenzy about the soul, we stand no chance at all to make her see that Jerutu is harmless and is in need of help.'

'I get you,' Grandpa agreed. 'I volunteer to talk to her about this in a calmer moment at a more conducive ambience.'

'Thanks, Grandpa,' Ronie said softly.

'My pleasure. Now hurry. Go after that face of smoke … Jerutu … before you lose it again. Meanwhile, Dunu and I will escort Hazel back into the house. Hurry!'

A frantic Hazel was still shouting and waving her hands in terror, calling out to every farmhand near or far, or even gone to the market, when Grandpa and Dunu arrived near her. And the two did and said whatever they thought might calm Hazel.

'Calm down, Hazel, calm down,' Grandpa said, 'that smoke face has come out of the house, hasn't it?'

'It has! It has! O my holy Buddha, it has!'

'Then doesn't it make more sense for us to get out of its way and go inside the house?'

'Why, yes, it sure does!' She turned around and still shrieking and talking simultaneously, ran towards the house with Dunu and Grandpa at her heels.

'Now, Hazel,' Dunu ran up from behind and caught hold of Hazel's hand, 'won't we just let the soul know where exactly we are if we shout and shriek like this? Won't it then be easy for the soul to come and get us?'

Hazel stopped in her tracks and looked at Dunu. Then she nodded vigorously. From growing up with Hazel, Dunu knew that the more vigorous her nods were, the more she agreed with whatever she was nodding for. She suddenly grabbed Dunu up in her arms, silently motioned Grandpa to follow her and ran into the house. Dunu looked at Grandpa over Hazel's shoulders and showed a thumbs-up. Grandpa winked. He turned once to look at the two palms standing erect on the highest point of Umata farm.

Could the nut that fell from one of them really be a link to his past? Like he always felt, deep in his heart?

❧

Outside in the farm, the hundredth Jerutu was still at large. But the oowii-oowiis didn't know where to look for it. And Vesak Poya was three days away. Just then, Ronie suddenly got all excited.

'Hey, look! Look at the dog! Look at his unusual behaviour!' he whispered.

'The dog be having name, Ronie, he be Brum. You be a-calling him that!' Sandie said with indignation.

'That's it! Yes, yes! It's there! The soul is there! A dog can sense the presence of souls!' Sunny squealed.

Brum was restless like never before. He jumped and ran after what seemed like an invisible butterfly, barking all the while. When Joyan walked up to him, he ran a few paces and returned to Joyan before again running ahead, as if he wanted Joyan to follow him. And now he was barking and sniffing into the huge cauldron, next to the horse stable. Joyan had already cooked in it the gruel-like fodder for the horses and sat it to cool before feeding them.

'Sshh, he may lead us to something. Just watch and follow the dog ... the ... Drum,' Sunny suggested.

'Brum!' Sandie corrected him.

They watched without making the slightest movement, lest they distracted Brum. Boy! How the oowii-oowiis heard their hearts thump loud even though they held their breath to stay still! They just had to find the Jerutu before Vesak Poya.

Soon Joyan appeared with a long, wrought-iron ladle.

'Ohoi Brum!' he called out, 'that gruel isn't yours, boy, now step aside.'

But Brum didn't step aside. Instead, he looked at Joyan and whimpered, growled, yawned aloud, purred and once even sneezed and burped, and made every possible noise that he could, touching the side of the cauldron with his paw every now and then.

'Let me stir that gruel. That will let out whatever little heat and steam that is trapped in there.' And Joyan went ahead and dipped the ladle into the fodder. The moment he stirred the ladle halfway round the cauldron, trapped steam indeed appeared above the fodder and it assembled itself to look like Brum's head with his snout. And the next thing the smoky Brum-head did was place a breezy, smoky, high-five with its smoky snout on Brum's moist, rubbery one!

'That's it, look! It is Jerutu! It is!' Sunny said excitedly.

But the high-five smack so immensely shocked Brum that the poor dog let out a terrible yelp followed by an equally pharynx-splitting bark which echoed all around the Kindoree valley. All this out-of-tune noise sent poor Jerutu into such intense a dread that it whiffed away towards the nearest vessel with fluid in it, which happened to be the large, shallow pan with water for the piglets.

Brum ran after Jerutu.

The oowii-oowiis ran after Brum.

A couple of piglets were already drinking from the pan. And happily, unaware, one of them slurped Jerutu in too, along with the water.

'Oh, shit!' Sunny exclaimed.

'Oh, shit!' Ronie repeated.

Because they all saw the smoke trailing into the piglet's mouth and yet could do nothing to stop it. Three days to go for Vesak Poya and now the hundredth Jerutu lay in a swine's gut.

'No shit,' Sandie garnered hope, 'I be a-climbing on to that the piglet with that the soul in his twirly intestines and be marking him. You boys be a-doing some whatever thing to pass that gas out of that pig's inside.' Saying so she ran towards the piglet without taking her eyes off it to keep a track of the piglet, so that it didn't get lost among the other pigs.

'Do what, Smarty Pants?' Sunny asked after her, infuriated.

'Some whatever thing!' she looked around and shouted.

But as she took her eyes off to look around at Sunny, the piglets moved and mingled, and Sandie lost track of the piglet that moved away with Jerutu in its innards.

'I know, it's that one on the right,' Ronie tried to help, 'or is it the one next to it?' he reconsidered, 'no, I guess it's the one up front…'

'I guess you don't know,' Sunny snapped.

'So?' Sandie questioned now, nervousness gripping them all over again.

'I know! Brum! Only he can sniff out the double-souled piglet,' Ronie suggested.

Brum was still sniffing by the water pan around which there were about twenty fidgeting and snorting pigs, three hysterical oowii-oowiis and one lost soul. And in that melee when Ronie, Sunny and the big dog suddenly came face to face, they just looked on at one another without any dramatic reaction, as if they had known one another since the beginning of time. They just happened to fall together into one and the same team that was trying to trace the lost soul.

Joyan had now fed the horses and was approaching the piglets.

'Ohoi hoi Brum boy!' he called out. Joyan always considered Brum as just another farm hand. Or farm-paw, for that matter. 'Now put that bark to good use and round up those piglets, will you? Namgyal must already be on his way. He'll take the piglets away now to sell them in the market early tomorrow morning.'

'No!' The oowii-oowiis looked at one another, horrified. 'Not again!'

Tashi Namgyal lived in the valley below and must have seen not more than fourteen or fifteen summers. But he had a way with animals. Sometimes the right way, sometimes the wrong way but a way, he surely had. He was amazing at herding cattle, and he was equally amazing at disbanding cattle, which were already herded. Tashi Namgyal never came alone. He was always accompanied by a slingshot, a pocketful of hardened yak-milk chewies and a small stick with a rope loop at the top. The stick with the loop hung from a large wooden button stitched onto a goat-skin belt decorated with cowry shells. Tashi Namgyal wore this belt not around his waist but slung over a shoulder and brought down across his front to the waist on the other side, over the green coat he always had on him. And so, the stick dangled from his waist and pointed down along his leg like a sword.

As Dunu put it, 'Tashi Namgyal's voice always reached before he did, that too in parts. Head first. Then chest. Then the top of the stick. And then the entire stick and the legs till the boy was whole. It was so because he walked up and up the slope from below till he arrived at the farm.'

So now they were all waiting for Tashi Namgyal to arrive in full.

Meanwhile, amidst the disarray that afternoon, Brum was shepherding the piglets which were going every other way except where they ought to.

'Foorrhii … farrhaa … far … r … r … h … a … a…!' Tashi Namgyal's voice appeared from below the mountain slopes.

Sunny immediately hopped up a tree to watch Tashi Namgyal appear.

That day, Tashi Namgyal's arms appeared before his head did. Because the arms were raised above his head, with the slingshot stretched in his hands and aimed at some bird up in the sky. And for pebbles on the slingshot, Tashi Namgyal always used the yak milk chewies. That was the reason why he carried these chewies.

'A … a … I … I … e … e…' he pulled hard at the rubber straps on the slingshot stretching them to their fullest, '… yaaa … a … a!' and let go. The yak-milk chewie bolted skywards.

Below, Brum was rounding up the piglets. And before the whole of Tashi Namgyal appeared, his yak-milk chewie fell from the skies and landed hard on the snout of a piglet. Startled and terrified, the poor piglet started running away from his assembled position. This led all other piglets too to disperse and they all started running amok till total chaos took over. Immediately, a great noise of snorting and squealing pigs, whistling and shouting people, sticks and ladles beating against cauldrons and clapping hands filled the Umata grounds.

At the stables, Barhonka, Poohor, and Botah too began to neigh and add to the mayhem. In their desperate effort to round up the piglets and restore order, Thapa, Minkai, Tashi, and Joyan bellowed at each other in languages never heard. They seemed to communicate solely by rolling and twisting their tongues and lips, while noisily letting out great volumes of air from the mouth.

As Sunny watched from his perch on the tree, he saw that everyone ran after the other, but no one exactly was sure of who was running after whom. A few piglets even ran towards the house, towards the kitchen door, to get inside and escape the bedlam. The only reason that Hazel was not out there chastising the piglets was that she was roasting fiery, cayenne pepper in the kitchen to add to a curry for supper. Its spicy aroma had been teasing her nostrils and every time she opened her mouth to shout at those outside, a forceful sneeze came and blew away all the babble out of her. She coughed and sneezed until her nose began to resemble a ripe tomato. The aroma of the pepper soon started to float out of the door and just as it entered Hazel's nostrils, so it did into the few piglets whose snouts were fast approaching the kitchen. But when the spice made them snort and sneeze into the kitchen, they immediately took a roundabout and once again ran out into the open.

By now, however, Tashi Namgyal appeared in whole and took charge of the piglets. He put away his slingshot and took the stick out of its peg and whirred it once in the air to announce the commencement of his task.

'Ka … khrrawm … khaang … haa…' he called out to the piglets. He breathed in a large amount of wind through his nostrils and made them roll noisily against the uvula dangling from the roof in his throat. In the process, he made a tremendous noise, something between a snort and a snore. The piglets understood instantly, calming down and huddling closer to one another. They had been herded, and soon they were gently guided down the slope.

'Oh, oh! There be go Jerutu a-hiking that a ride in some a-pig gut!' Sandie shouted, jumping up and down in dismay.

'Stop! Stop!' Sunny raced down the tree, screaming, and ran after the piglets and back to Ronie and Sandie, and again towards the piglets. His thatch roof rose and fell in harmony with his running back and forth. The oowii-oowiis were distraught. Ronie ran up to Brum who was now sitting on his hinds with his tongue merrily hanging out. He was watching the piglets go away, glad to have done his work of herding satisfactorily and, well, completely forgetting about a certain soul he was chasing.

'You stub of a muzzle! You!' Ronie shouted at Brum, 'use that snout and go find out the piglet with Jerutu in it, can't you? Go!'

Brum joyfully thumped his tail on the ground, stood up and was all set to obey to the command. Only, he was waiting for a stick to be hurled. Ronie sighed and sat down, crestfallen.

'That which is destined to be, will yet be,' he repeated Old Monk's words.

12

Grandpa Shares His Past

Distraught and wondering what to do about the lost Jerutu, the oowii-oowiis stared into the descending night. The sky was slowly turning into a dark shade of indigo. Speckled with tiny stars, it was beginning to look like a gorgeous, sequined cloak of dark blue satin, with the radiant moon pinned upon it like a brooch of gold. It was almost filling up into a wholesome circle. Almost. From his balcony, Girim Umata and Dunu were also staring at the same moon. But the beauty of the night sky failed to gladden their hearts. Instead, the moon in it was causing all of them inconceivable magnitudes of anxiety.

'Just two days left for Vesak Poya, Grandpa,' Dunu said, still looking at the moon. She expected Grandpa to reply. He didn't. She never saw him so distant, immersed and so melancholic. She tried again. 'We still haven't found the Jerutu.'

He still didn't reply.

'In which case, can we just let the Jerutu be? But then again, without it, how will the ninety-nine other Jerutus receive emancipation?' She tried one more time.

This time Grandpa spoke, but his voice bore the ache in his heart. 'I don't know about the ninety-nine other Jerutus but I think I know about the hundredth Jerutu.'

'You do?' Dunu asked, surprised.

'I'm not sure but I think I do.'

He looked up at the moon. A fluff of cloud sailed across it. And because the cloud was sailing south-west, he knew it would soon arrive over the sky at Fhuwanji. This thought awakened in him a need to talk about his past. Of Fhuwanji. Of Keihoong and Neishri. Of Pholey Deehang. Most of all, of Baulungbwrai.

'Child, do you remember your ma and papa?'

Dunu didn't know how to respond to this and remained quiet. The impression she always had was that mas and papas belonged to her friends in school. For her, there was Grandpa. And Hazel.

'I have them?' she asked.

'You did.'

'Where?'

Girim Umata led his little grandchild to his room and sat her on his bed. He then walked to his wardrobe, opened it and dug deep behind his coats on the top shelf. From there, he pulled out a small, wooden box with intricate floral carvings all over it. Still carrying it close to his heart with one hand, he pulled his rocking chair towards Dunu with the other. He sat down on it with such a deep sigh that it seemed like the load of the box pressed to his heart was insufferable. That moment, he was planning to unburden it all. He would share. He didn't know how much little Dunu would understand though. He wanted to wait until she grew older, but destiny had its own plans. He opened the box with much love and brought out an old photograph, placed carefully in the folds of soft linen. It was turning yellow and crisp at the edges. He looked long at it.

'Who are those people, Grandpa?' Dunu asked, leaning forward to rest her elbow on the arm of the rocking chair to look at the photograph. Grandpa put the photograph in her hand.

'She's a beautiful woman, isn't she?' Dunu said, touching the woman in the picture lightly with her fingers.

'She is, child, as beautiful as you are. She's your ma. Neishri.'

Dunu stared at the picture. 'And that's papa?' she asked.

Grandpa nodded without looking at her or the picture. Because he didn't want her to see the tears in his eyes.

'And why is ma carrying that little bundle of clothes? Hey wait! That's a baby! I guess that's me?' Now she jumped off the bed.

Grandpa nodded again. He didn't want her eyes to meet his. He didn't want her to see the weaker, vulnerable side of her grandpa. He instead walked towards the window, drew the curtain aside and looked at the moon.

'You must be seeing Fhuwanji as well from up there, moon, and also the Bathou temple,' he thought.

Hazel appeared at that moment with a bowl of steaming chicken and mint soup for Dunu. 'There you go, child, now this will keep all the sneezes and trickly nose at bay, and you will...'

'Hey, Hazel, look at this. My ma and papa!' Dunu held out the picture towards Hazel.

Hazel looked at it with great interest. And now that the matter was touched, she too showed a desire to know about Dunu's parents. In all these ten years of her stay at the Umata household, she never once broached this matter, out of respect for Girim Umata's feelings of not wishing to talk about the past. But today, Grandfather wished to speak. The rest wished to listen.

'Ahem, I apologize, Grandpa, but if I may be allowed to ask, where are they? Dunu's ma and papa?' Hazel asked, scared she might hurt his feelings.

Grandpa replied, 'You may ask, Hazel, you may. Because I too need to tell. But before that,' he was still staring out of the window into the night sky, 'get me my mug so I can pour myself some good ale to infuse courage in me. I need immense strength to speak of what I have been trying to keep buried deep here,' and he tapped on his heart, 'and Hazel, don't stop or discipline me on my ale today.'

Even if Grandpa would not have mentioned it, Hazel would still have the kindness and good sense to keep quiet about his ale that evening. Because her heart was as large as her presence, with enough room to carry the pains and feelings of those around her, she went out and returned almost immediately with his mug.

'Here's your mug, Grandpa, and I've placed a few slices of bacon on the pan. I'll get them as soon as they are done.'

'So where are Ma and Papa?' Dunu asked. 'Can they help us find Jerutu?'

Grandpa poured himself a generous help from his bottle of ale and took a sip.

'I don't know. Though my heart tells me there is definitely a link. For it's been ten years, as Old Monk estimates, since the Jerutu came away or was made to come away from the precincts of Shiva and has been looking for someone it shared a deep bond with. And it's been exactly that many years since the great floods at Fhuwanji, when the Dwisikhlaa swelled abruptly and ravenously.' Grandpa paused. He went back to looking at the moon outside. 'Dwisikhlaa swept away my Keihoong and Neishri that night, Dunu, your ma and papa.' He took a big gulp from the mug and stood silent for a while. The ache of all these past years came rushing upon him. Hazel and Dunu remained as quiet as the night, and as reassuring as the mountains outside. When Grandpa regained his composure, he turned to walk back and sit down on his rocking chair. Then he gradually told them about Baulungbwrai and the joukhoorei, and how the two were inseparable.

'Baulungbwrai!' Grandfather's eyes shone with fondness as he said the name. 'Ah, crazy old man! Never was young, never was awake. He was by Bathou and Bathou, at Fhuwanji, was by him. We had been hearing this story since we were little children ... that the day Baulungbwrai goes missing from the temple, great change will come over Fhuwanji's destiny. That flood that night,' he gulped hard, 'took away Baulungbwrai and great change did indeed come over Fhuwanji, and over everyone there; and over me. I left my homeland because I had to nurture Keihoong and Neishri's love, Hazel, I had to nurture Dunu, who was only an infant then. My inseparable friend, Pholey Deehang, got separated from me. I don't know how he is now just as I don't know how Fhuwanji is. And the Bathou temple there.

I don't know what will restore Fhuwanji; or Baulungbwrai, or the soul in his joukhoorei. Because both were merged into one. I don't know if it is one of them that Old Monk says is instinctively gravitating towards the other. If it is, could your lost spirit be the soul in the joukhoorei? Could it be the one Old Monk says is the hundredth Jerutu?' Girim Umata paused. He took another sip. 'The old at Fhuwanji, who probably are no more now, also said that the soul in the joukhoorei always kept the joukhoorei full, as long as someone, the same person, kept drinking from it. Baulungbwrai used to do that, from the joukhoorei that housed the soul. That's how the soul and Baulungbwrai shared this deep and unique bond.'

'Sorry to interrupt, Grandpa, but please give me a moment so I can hurry and get the bacon.' And Hazel dashed to the kitchen to get the bacon. She even stumbled over her flying apron in her hurry. 'Now don't you come in the way!' she admonished it, 'you're Hazel's apron, and no queen's cloak, pah!' and she scurried away to the kitchen and back, lest Grandpa continued with his tale without her. In the meantime, Grandpa walked over to pour himself some more ale. He opened the bottle and had just placed its cork on the cabinet, when Hazel arrived with sizzling slices of bacon with dollops of home-made cheese melting on them. Dunu ran forward to pick one for herself. When she looked well to see which one to pick, she thought a part of the steam looked somewhat different. Instead of gently swaying upwards and away, the steam seemed to be coiling itself to impersonate a round slice of bacon.

'Jerutu?' she wondered. 'Couldn't be. He's gone with the piglet.' But before she could take another good look and be sure, it mingled with the rest of the sizzle and steam, and vanished. Dunu was sure she had an illusion because she had been constantly thinking of where and how to find the Jerutu. Grandpa poured his ale and held up the bottle to see how low the level of ale fell in the bottle. Two-thirds and a little more. That much he had drunk up that evening.

'The last for today,' he told Hazel, raising his mug as he picked up two slices of bacon with the fork.

She smiled and nodded.

'Dunu, child, I am definite the hola-holas said it was Bathou that Old Monk referred to Shiva as, wasn't it?'

'Bathou, yeah. Hola-hola, no! Oowii-oowii,' she corrected him.

'Bathou, that's what we call Shiva in Fhuwanji, Hazel. Anyone around here or down in the valley, in your Kindoree, calls Shiva as Bathou?'

'Without another moment's consideration and with conviction, Grandpa, no one,' Hazel promptly replied, 'no village. Till far, far away from here and from Kindoree.' She felt immensely important and intelligent to be able to give such useful information with such clarity and instantly.

'When I left Fhuwanji with Dunu, when I passed by the Bathou temple those ten years ago, I saw Baulungbwrai's joukhoorei hanging upon the erect stone structure we worshipped as Bathou. And now I am confused,' he once again walked up to the window, 'if the joukhoorei is still there, could the soul be there as well? Or might it have been empty since that night?'

'But, Grandpa,' Dunu told him, 'if what the old folks then said about the soul remaining there only as long as someone drank from it, and if there is no sipping from it because there is no Baulungbwrai there anymore, how could the soul be there?'

Little children's uncomplicated minds saw things so much more clearly and with such assurance. It was well past Dunu's bedtime but that evening, time itself seemed to have gone back. Everyone forgot about supper and bedtime. Grandpa picked up the photograph from the bed and lovingly looked at it for a while before putting it into the folds of the linen and placing it back into the wooden box. Then he put the box away in his wardrobe, closed it and returned to sit on his chair, pensive and confused.

That evening Grandpa and Dunu also told Hazel about Old Monk and the Dendup Gompa and why Owl had sent the oowii-oowiis there.

'So, you see, Hazel,' Grandpa picked up another slice of bacon though the cheese had cooled off by then, 'how could creatures who have been expected at, and who have visited the sacrosanct grounds of Dendup Gompa, ever be the devil in disguise? How could they be beings of the dark, Hazel? Is it even remotely possible, tell me?'

Hazel nodded. Very slowly though. Dunu giggled into her palm because she could make out how much Hazel agreed, from the pathetically low intensity of her nod.

'As for the soul,' Grandpa continued, 'if it has lived long in the precincts of Shiva, how on earth, dear Hazel, how on earth can it be evil? If it is expected to pave the way for the emancipation of ninety-nine exalted and purified souls, Hazel, nirvana as you call it, how on earth can it be evil? It is rather more virtuous than you or me, eh? Think, Hazel, think. And if you can help the hola-holas…'

'Oowii-oowiis,' Dunu corrected him.

'Yes them,' Grandpa went on, 'and the lost soul of the joukhoorei…'

'If it is ever found, that is,' Dunu chipped in.

'Yes, if it is ever found, that is, you will only earn the Buddha's grace, Hazel, that you will.'

Grandpa, Hazel, and Dunu were reminded of time by Brum. He appeared in their midst only to walk up to Hazel, as if to remind her that it was long past his suppertime. Then he walked up to the cabinet where the bottle of ale stood, sniffed at it, and returned to Hazel. Rubbing his side against her legs, he looked up at her and whimpered softly.

'He's hungry, Hazel,' Dunu interpreted.

'Oh dear! Whatever is happening to me?' Hazel got up with a start, suddenly coming out of a reverie. 'First I leave Dunu hungry and then I leave the big boy hungry. Have mercy, my Buddha, show me mercy!'

'He will,' Grandpa smiled, 'he has already shown you an opportunity to earn his mercy.'

'Hmm. Er … yes. Come now, I will lay supper for you two as well,' and she called Dunu and Grandpa away for supper, while sleepy Brum dragged himself after her.

13

'We've Found Jerutu!'

Girim Umata couldn't sleep that night. It was a feeling of remorse that kept him awake. Because he had failed to take care of the soul that destiny brought to his farm, entrusting him with the responsibility of restoring it to where it belonged. And if it truly was the lost soul of the joukhoorei, maybe Girim Umata was also entrusted with the responsibility of restoring Fhuwanji. Or, of mediating the soul's transportation to the Tree of Emancipation, so that the hundred Jerutus could be liberated from the cycle of rebirth. But he had failed.

It was also a feeling of anxiety and panic that kept him awake. There were only two more days before Vesak Poya, but the lost soul was yet to be traced.

'Calm, calm,' he told himself, 'the soul may yet be found. Let us not see only two more days. Let us instead see two days more. That's quite some time.' He hoped to take

Brum all around Umata farm at the break of dawn so that he could help find the soul. But the thought of finding the soul suddenly made him go weak in the knees.

'What if it is the same soul that is destined to restore Fhuwanji and to liberate the ninety-nine Jerutus, that too on the night of Vesak Poya?' A sudden bout of restlessness gripped his heart. A hot flush numbed his head, and a cold shudder reached down his spine to freeze his feet. 'Which should it be if such a situation arises? Fhuwanji or the nirvana of the souls?' he wondered, hoping such a situation never arose. 'Of course, Fhuwanji!' he thought, walking up to the window and looking at the moon. It had moved higher into the sky now.

'Fhuwanji!' Grandpa reassured himself.

He walked back to the rocking chair and slumped down on it, exhausted like never before. Too many thoughts were forcing into his mind all at once.

'But the soul, without Baulungbwrai, will not remain in the joukhoorei. It will escape again. I must search for Baulungbwrai instead. But, no! I must first meet Pholey Deehang. I must go to Fhuwanji. But I don't know if even a pathetic fragment of Fhuwanji survived that flood. Or whether Dwisikhlaa had once again changed course and Fhuwanji is already restored. Oh dear! I don't understand this mystery, Lord, I can't think anymore!'

Girim Umata shut his eyes and let his head fall back onto the headrest of the chair. No moral dilemma ever hit him this hard. He tried to rock himself to sleep on the chair, but sleep would not come. He got up and walked out to the veranda. The breeze was cold outside. He braced himself yet he heard his teeth chatter. All around him, the Umata farmlands rolled out into the darkness, oblivious to his angst. From where he stood in the veranda, he could see the two coconut palms rising into the night sky, their fronds glorious like crowns, shimmering in the moonlight. It amazed him that he had always felt they would bring him news of Fhuwanji someday. And they eventually did too. But Girim Umata didn't expect the news to come in such a confusing and traumatizing manner. He didn't expect the news to leave him feeling that it would have been better, had there been no news at all.

He was left with greater misery now than before, since word from Fhuwanji arrived. Word, in the form of a soul. Beyond the farmlands, the lofty mountains stood quiet and peaceful, almost god themselves. Invincible, yet so benevolent. Embracing all who sought refuge in them. They accepted Girim Umata too, when he arrived there years ago. So now too he looked at them with hope, that they would grant him solace and a way out from the confusion.

He slowly walked back to his room and made his way to the cabinet. He desperately needed another mug of ale. When he brought out the bottle of ale from the cabinet, it felt heavy. When he raised the bottle to eye level and looked into it nice and well, he staggered with astonishment. The bottle was full!

'Jerutu? Could it be? It has to be him! O dear Lord! I know it is Jerutu! Filling up my bottle as he did Baulungbwrai's joukhoorei!' he spoke aloud out of thrill.

He held the bottle up and looked at it once again to be sure. The bottle was indeed full. He was getting restless to break the news to Dunu. To the oowii-oowiis. To Owl. To Hazel. But he also wanted to let them all get some sleep. He was beside himself with excitement now and at the same time, all the more confused and torn apart. What if it is indeed the same soul?

Will it then be Fhuwanji?

Or emancipation of the hundred Jerutus?

Girim Umata didn't notice when the soft spray of vermilion touched the eastern sky. It was already dawn. He hadn't had a wink of sleep all night. He went inside, woke Dunu, and told her about the mysteriously refilled ale bottle. She tossed aside the blankets and jumped out of bed immediately. Brum, who was lying beside the bed, didn't approve of being woken so early and openly expressed his displeasure. Yet, he knew he had to get up and move, for without him, nothing worked right on the Umata farm.

'I thought I saw Jerutu last evening, Grandpa … that smoke over the bacon slices! Yes, I know! Yeah!' Dunu's words tumbled over each other in her excitement.

What she—and everyone else—didn't know was that the piglet, who had sneezed into the kitchen door after inhaling the smell of roasted chilies, had also sneezed Jerutu out of its system and back into the Umata house. Jerutu had then wandered around the kitchen, looking for a vessel with fluid. Spotting the jar of oil, he slipped into it. When Hazel poured him out into the pan and dropped the bacon slices on top, Jerutu found his way onto the tray, travelling with the bacon and cheese to Grandpa's room. From there, he made his way into Grandpa's bottle of ale when it was left open to refill his mug.

Dunu rushed out onto her balcony, barefoot and bare-headed. Cold was the last thing she felt in that moment.

'Sandie! Ronie! Sunny! Owl! It's Jerutu!' She cupped her palms around her mouth like a megaphone to let her voice reach out to wherever the oowii-oowiis and Owl might be.

'WE'VE FOUND JERUTU!' she shouted out in great delight.

Grandpa suddenly wished they hadn't found Jerutu. His mind now staggered between the decision to bind the soul to earthly attachments or to liberate it. But since the hundredth Jerutu had already been found, he desperately wished it would not be the same one that had been lost from the joukhoorei. And yet, that too seemed almost certain.

By now, the farm had woken to another new day and was buzzing with activity. Grandpa and Dunu sat on the swing outside the kitchen, contemplating their next course of action. Owl flew in, circled around them, and perched on one of the swing's posts. Soon, the oowii-oowiis appeared like a merry gust of wind.

'Isn't this the brightest morning ever, Grandpa?' Sunny hopped excitedly all over the swing.

Ronie couldn't help but crow, his excitement bubbling over. 'So, where is it? The smoke blob? Where?' He jerked his weathercock this way and that, hoping for a sudden burst of smoke to reward him with a playful high-five.

'Grandpa? Dunu?' Sandie bounced about, barely able to contain her joy. 'We're missing the adorable smoke, Dunu, heh heh! It's stealing our hearts, right, Sunny? Ronie?' The boys grinned, their eyes glowing.

And then they heard Hazel. She was coming towards the swing alright, her voice preceding her. Brum followed her, trying to get at her apron strings.

'Aiyaa! Some joyous congregation this, eh?' Even she seemed to beam with relief and joy.

'Oh! But, Grandpa!' A frown was suddenly beginning to form between her eyebrows. 'Why is that bottle of ale in your hands this early in the morning?'

Grandpa looked down at the bottle in his hands. His eyes looked disturbed. Sunny skipped close to Ronie and nudged him with his tail. The oowii-oowiis noticed that Grandpa didn't seem as delighted as they all were.

'Uh, Grandpa?' Owl flew down closer to Girim Umata.

'Jerutu slumbers in this bottle of ale here,' Grandpa announced.

The congregation fell silent. All eyes turned towards the bottle.

'So now tell me, hola-holas,' Grandpa spoke after a long silence.

'Oowii-oowiis,' Sandie corrected.

'Ah yes! I keep forgetting, excuse my silliness please. So then tell me, hola-holas, what exactly did Old Monk tell you about the soul?'

'He referred to it as … mmm … lost,' Sunny recollected.

'And he asked if it came from any fluid in a vessel,' Ronie added.

'Jou in the joukhoorei,' Grandpa quietly confirmed to himself.

'Are you sure Old Monk really said a decade? About the time span it's been lost?' he asked.

'Oh yes!' Sunny confirmed.

'Lost during that devastating flood a decade ago,' Grandpa added another piece of the puzzle.

'And yes! Old Monk be saying, Jerutu be looking for and a-coming close to be with one somebody he many years be a-living with, some long time ago … a decade be. That be years a-ten, eh?' Sandie said.

'Is the soul coming close to be with Bathou in the mountains? In Shiva's abode, Kailash?' Grandpa thought to himself. But when he spoke, he found himself asking something else. 'Old Monk said Bathou?'

'He did,' Sunny confirmed once more.

There was a moment of silence but a moment which seemed like an eternity. Every piece in the puzzle of the lost soul of the joukhoorei was falling into place, one after the other. By now they all were definite about the soul, but none mustered the courage to speak it out. And then Hazel slowly stepped forward.

'Grandpa,' she said softly, not to give him a rude jolt of the truth, 'it indeed is the same soul. It is the lost soul of the joukhoorei and also the hundredth Jerutu.'

Dunu looked at Grandpa. He never looked so lost and defeated. He had hoped against hope that they weren't the same soul. Truth, when it hurt to the core, is difficult to accept. Even when one knew that it was but the whole truth. Just so, Girim Umata was now terrified to face it although he knew the truth and the truth was that it was the same soul. He got up from the swing and walked a little distance away, from where he could see the palm trees. The only ones in the whole of Kindoree. Was this too a play of destiny?

'If only I could get one glimpse of Fhuwanji, if only I knew whether it is still there,' he rued. However much he tried to veil it, the rest could hear the quiver in his voice, and the sniffle.

'We have one night and one day before the Vesak Poya moon rises. May I volunteer to fly out there, to Fhuwanji, and get that glimpse for you, Grandpa?' Owl offered. 'Allow me to be your eyes.'

Grandpa looked at Owl gratefully, and then at Dunu and Hazel. The girls agreed in unison. Hazel nodded so vigorously that the scarf from her head threatened to come off.

'That'll actually be helpful, won't it?' Sunny asked no one in particular.

'Owl, thank you,' was all Grandpa managed to say.

'Tonight then?' Ronie asked Owl.

'At dusk,' Owl replied. 'I'll be back before dawn tomorrow. Here by the swing.'

'Whichever way it is, we will have to take Jerutu to where he belongs, Grandpa, so where does he belong? How do we take him there?' Dunu asked.

Now they all wanted to hear what Grandpa had decided. He walked back to the swing and sat next to Dunu. He sat long and thought hard.

'On one hand, Fhuwanji's revival was not assured even if the soul was put back into its joukhoorei. Fhuwanji might resurface, it might not. If it did, it would be like the phoenix. But if it didn't? Then having found the lost soul would be futile. Moreover, there would be no second chance for the soul to serve either of its twin purposes. But on the other hand, the emancipation of the hundred Jerutus was assured.'

Girim Umata decided not to gamble with destiny, for he had already lost enough. He picked Dunu gently onto his lap and embraced her close, as if he needed her support once again like he did a decade ago when he left Fhuwanji, with little Dunu pressed to his bosom.

That was then. He let go of Fhuwanji.

This was now. He would once more let go of Fhuwanji. He broke then. And healed.

He was breaking now. He didn't know if he would ever heal.

'We take him to Dendup Gompa,' Grandpa said slowly, as he buried his face in Dunu's embrace and sobbed.

They never saw the jolly old man thus shaken with grief. The oowii-oowiis came and sat at his feet. Hazel came close and stood behind him while Owl flew down to sit on Grandpa's otherwise strong and able shoulders. Brum crawled closer and put his chin on grandpa's knee. Silently, and in their own way, they stood by him when they thought he needed them; they stood by the one whom they all came to love and revere as their grandpa, the one who had always been their answer to every question, who had a solution to every problem; the one whom they turned to for strength and succour. Now though, that same grandpa was breaking down. They all sat with him in silence, letting him sob and share his pain with them.

When Hazel heard a cough and turned around, she saw that Joyan, Minkai, Kelman and Thapa too had come to be by Grandpa at that moment when they felt he needed their support. Girim Umata never felt so intensely loved and belonged, since the night of the devouring floods. Every tear they shed for Grandpa and every touch of their assurance made him sob even louder. He wanted to bring all of them into his embrace. He wanted to cry aloud. He wanted to run back all the way down the mountains to have a last glance of the place that was once Fhuwanji. But all he did instead was hold tighter to Dunu. She felt him shaking all over as he sobbed into her. Even though her little heart broke to feel his sobs, she held him close and lay her head on his, as if on behalf of every creature, big and small, that waited with Grandpa at that fateful moment by the swing. Taking the decision shattered his heart into pieces, but all those beautiful beings around him, human, animal, bird and insect, made it less hard. They even made it bearable.

And Grandpa knew he would heal once again.

14

Preparations for Jerutu's Journey

That whole day, Girim Umata kept to himself. He had made his decision, and now there was no turning back. It wasn't easy though. His decision would affect every villager of Fhuwanji, who had for generations lived all their lives in that village, until the night of the deluge. Some, like Pholey Deehang, might have harboured hopes of returning, whenever and if ever Fhuwanji was restored. Girim Umata would be answerable to each of them. To Pholey Deehang. To Bawlungbwrai, if he was ever found. Had he placed the souls he didn't even know, to which he had no attachment, above his own people? Had he made the right choice? Girim Umata paced around his room, repeating the question to himself. Had he done right? A couple of times, he stopped near the cabinet and took a sip from his bottle of ale. Each time, he would return to the bottle, holding it up to check if it had refilled. Sure enough, after every sip, the level rose back to the brim. Restlessness gnawed at him, waiting for Owl to return to the post of the swing in the vegetable patch by the kitchen, back from his journey to Fhuwanji.

At the same time, Girim Umata struggled with how to transfer the Jerutu from his bottle of ale into another vessel with a different fluid. He couldn't bring himself to carry ale through the sacred threshold of Buddha's abode at the gompa, especially not during Vesak Poya. Yet, his mind refused to focus, as stray memories interrupted his thoughts. Though irrelevant now, they still connected him to his roots. There was the annual harvest festival at the Bathou temple, when every family participated. Then there was the time when a monkey had piddled on Pholey Deehang during a community hunting trip. A sad smile crossed Girim Umata's face as he remembered the scar left on Pholey Deehang's cheek, below his left temple. He thought of the time they had rescued an injured elephant calf, and the village had united to reunite it with its herd. There was also the time when every able-bodied youth had come together to construct the embankment along Dwisikhlaa.

Girim Umata and Pholey Deehang had been strong, muscled youths back then, toiling away with pride. But now, as he tried to process these memories, his mind remained clouded.

Grandpa went out and walked towards the old tool shed near the quarters of the farm hands. It was there that Thapa put iron soles onto the hoofs of Barhonka, Poohor, and their now grown daughter Botah. In these ten years, Barhonka and Poohor had added a handsome, brown son to their family. Because in Creation, whatever the calamity, birth and thereby life, never came to a pause. Dunu had named him Niyor. In the same shed, Thapa greased and mended the wheels of the horse carts and the wheelbarrows and bent straight rods of iron to make rakes during autumn. It was there that Thapa stored all kinds of bric-a-brac, some of which were absolutely of no use. But Thapa always felt that two useless things put together might yet result in the making of one useful thing. So, Grandpa let him reign over this shed.

Now as he inspected this shed well, high and low, he saw that it was in a complete mess. But it was one place which could be made smoke tight, by removing all the stuff and by nailing narrow planks to close the splits on the sideboards. The roof, though low, was steady and needed no reinforcement. The shed, Grandpa decided, was the only place that could be made ready for transferring the hundredth Jerutu from one vessel of fluid to another. The shed was also just the right size to hold the oowii-oowiis, Hazel, Dunu and Grandpa and of course, the all-important bottle of ale, all at the same time. So, Grandpa and Thapa got down to readying the shed for the epoch-making transfer. However, Grandpa still couldn't think of what other vessel they could get Jerutu to enter, and how to take him to the gompa.

That afternoon as Hazel waited upon Dunu and Grandpa over lunch, he discussed the matter with them.

'Whatever it is, it has to be airtight,' he said.

'Like where Hazel stores my cookies?' Dunu interrupted, raising an eyebrow.

'Ssshh, listen up! And don't cheat on that spinach,' Hazel warned Dunu.

Grandpa resumed, 'I need to uncork that bottle of ale and leave it thus, till we see a smoke face swaggering out of it and swagger into what airtight container, I still haven't been able to figure that out.'

'Hmm … but that vessel should also have fluid in it, remember, Grandpa? Jerutu cannot go too far with the wind,' Dunu reminded him.

'Yes! I know what, Grandpa,' Hazel hit upon an idea. 'Milk! Because Jerutu got into that milk jar in the kitchen, remember? So, he'll take to milk. Maybe we should carry milk in a can to the gompa. We can offer it for the sweetened rice they prepare for the pilgrims in these h-u-u-g-e vessels.' She stretched the word huge to match the time of her spreading arms out wide till they reached as far behind as she could extend them, to indicate the hugeness of the vessels. 'And we can carry Jerutu in our milk can, eh?'

'Oh yeah, eh!' Dunu looked up, wincing over a bite of spinach, 'and pour Jerutu into the vessel T-H-I-S big,' she mimicked Hazel and stretched out her own arms this time to reach as far behind as she could, 'to let him be cooked and sucked once again into the gut of some pilgrim? No way, Hazel, we'll have to think up of something else!'

'Hey! There *is* a way here actually!' Grandpa's eyes brightened, like they did whenever he hit upon a solution. 'If we can manage to make Jerutu enter one of our milk cans, we can carry the can to the gompa and instead of giving it for the sweetened rice, we can hand it over to Old Monk. Old Monk will know what to do from there on.'

'But, Grandpa, if the milk isn't for the sweetened rice and is just to serve as a medium for Jerutu, why carry such a big can? It can be carried in a bottle as well, a bottle the size of your ale bottle,' Hazel suggested.

'Hey, but of course! You are wise, Hazel, we shall do so then. However, since we did think of making offerings for the sweetened rice, let that be done too. Let us carry two vessels of milk. A can for the real offering and a bottle, with Jerutu, for Old Monk. Now the concern is, how do we get that wind to pass onto the milk bottle?' Grandpa wondered aloud, furrows deepening on his forehead.

'Pass the wind to me,' Dunu said excitedly.

'What!' Hazel glared at Dunu. 'Now, dear child, stop being obscene, will you!'

'Huh? Oh! I didn't intend to mean what you think it to be, Hazel, I only meant, leave that wind … that Jerutu … to me. The oowii-oowiis know how to make Jerutu get into places they want it to.'

'Great. Then speak to the hola-holas about it. Let's get started. Every passing minute leaves us with a minute behind in this race against the Vesak Poya moon.' Grandpa signalled the go-ahead.

'Oowii-owiis,' Dunu corrected him for the umpteenth time.

'Then maybe we can ride Barhonka and Poohor to the gompa. Early tomorrow morning then, after Owl arrives. Okay with you girls?' he asked.

'Okay with me!' Hazel and Dunu said instantly and at the same moment. Dunu got out of her chair and gave Hazel a tight hug. Hazel smiled and held Dunu in her embrace as long as the little girl wanted to remain there.

'So, Hazel, get the milk and the milk bottle ready while I go and check on Thapa's work. Dunu, go child, gather up the hola-holas.'

'Oowii-oowiis.'

'Yes them, whatever. Right away! And let them too into the plan so far. If the shed is done, it'd be good if we shift Jerutu before sundown. We cannot risk another gassy escapade at this eleventh hour.' Grandpa pushed back his chair and got up. 'Get going then. We've got lots to do and little time.'

❧

Thapa had done his job well. He had emptied out the tool shed, sealed the splits and fixed the door so that it could be latched from inside. He had also mended the lone lantern and hung it from the ceiling. Grandpa made sure that there was no fluid whatsoever inside the shed. As he stood inside and inspected it thoroughly, he wondered how Ronie, Sunny, Sandie and Dunu would play their parts of passing the gas from the bottle of ale to the bottle of milk.

'But Dunu seemed confident. I'll leave the job to them,' Grandpa thought. He began to trust the fun-loving oowii-oowiis and Dunu, more. He then walked over to Thapa to instruct him further. 'Saddle and prepare Barhonka and Poohor, my boy, at the crack of dawn tomorrow we shall leave for Dendup Gompa on Mount Swrang.'

'To be at the Vesak Poya celebration, Grandpa?' the boy asked.

'Yes, yes. A pilgrimage of sorts, you see.'

What Grandpa hadn't realized was that it indeed was a pilgrimage, of a much higher order though. He had given up on the interests of the self for those of a greater good, a good that would liberate hundreds and thousands of sanctified souls.

'I will need you to come with us, Thapa,' Grandpa told him.

Thapa grinned wide as he nodded. He was too happy to be asked, and happier to say yes.

'And yes, we shall carry a can of milk as well. Ask Joyan to keep the milk ready before dawn. And now if you are done with the shed, go run along to finish up with your remaining chores before the daylight fades.'

Grandpa walked back to the house to fetch the bottle of ale and was even back before Hazel could say oowii-oowiis.

As soon as Thapa moved away, Dunu moved into the shed with Sandie, Sunny and Ronie. Soon Hazel too arrived with her bottle of milk. Without further ado and in silence, they all entered the tool shed and Grandpa locked the door from inside.

Tension, adrenaline, and pulses raced. Each thought the one nearest to him heard his heart go lub-dub-lub-dub way too loud and way too fast. Outside the shed, the late-afternoon sun played on for a while longer. Pumpkins growing on the ground looked rounder and a brighter shade of orange in the glow of the setting sun. The sound of bleating sheep and their copper bells swam in from afar. But inside the shed, all of this was abruptly cut off, as if a pair of scissors had snipped the farm away from the wooden boards that formed the shed's walls. Daylight had come to an abrupt halt just outside the wooden planks, just as did all farm sounds. Because even the most famished gaps along the wood wall had been sealed, lest Jerutu escaped through it. Like it did once from Dunu's drawer through the tiny opening that the mouse had made. Hazel never found out that there actually was a mouse in there that day, which nibbled out a wee gap in the sideboards of the drawer, through which Jerutu escaped before Hazel saw the coconut.

Now, however, Grandpa fumbled in the dark inside the shed for his bottle of ale.

'But there's a problem here,' Ronie's voice floated in the dark, 'we can't see a thing. We don't know where the bottle of milk is. We won't see Jerutu either.'

It was just one problem, but a big one.

'If only we had a matchbox,' Grandpa regretted, after all the details he bothered to look into. 'I know there's a lantern hanging from up here somewhere,' and he probably raised his hand to find it, because everyone heard something clank above their heads.

'Ah yes! It's here. But we have nothing to light it with. All of you wait back here while I hurry to the house and get a matchbox,' Grandpa said and slowly started to feel his way towards the door. All through this fuss, Hazel was furiously digging into the numerous pockets stitched onto every thinkable space on her apron, hoping to fish out a matchbox.

'No need, Grandpa, here, I've found one!' she proclaimed triumphantly, producing a matchbox from a pocket, forcing it out through a chock-a-block clutter of objects. In the process, a whole lot of other things too fell out of the pocket, of which some jingled and some plonked before landing on the hard earthen floor of the shed, while yet others went thud and bounced away in the dark. All this thudding, jingling and plonking vibrated along the ground and reached Brum, wherever he was on the farm. But to Hazel, all that fallen stuff didn't matter now. Even if they did, she had no time to pick them up.

Instead, she lit a matchstick and reached out for the lantern. And at last, there was light in the shed. And quiet, though just for a moment.

'Okay, Hazel, when Sunny raises his tail, remove the cap on the bottle of milk and leave it that way,' Ronie explained the strategy, 'and no one will make any unnecessary noise. Grandpa, uncork the bottle of ale when we signal you to do so.'

'Right!' Grandpa said obediently.

'Right!' said Hazel.

'Hmm? Yeah, right,' Dunu added.

A chill and a silent tension of such an enormous proportion began to simmer inside the small tool shed that Grandpa worried, if they didn't hurry with the proceedings, the walls of the shed would explode any minute. Dunu wondered if anybody even breathed. Lest she missed out on the signal, Hazel stared so hard at Sunny's tail without blinking that the poor squirrel got understandably nervous and forgot what he was supposed to do with his tail. Seconds and minutes ticked away but Sunny was yet to raise his tail. Hazel could hold the suspense no longer.

'Here now, you with the sun-dried thatch roof! Raise that tail of yours!' Hazel only whispered but it sounded like thunder in that stillness.

Zap! In an instant the tail was up.

Hazel uncapped the bottle of milk. Ronie, Sunny and Sandie fell into a neat row to do the same trick they successfully did on two earlier occasions, to put Jerutu into a definite place of their choice. The first time it was to put Jerutu into Owl's hollow and the second time, it was to put Jerutu back into the coconut. And now, Dunu squat on the floor next to them and Ronie looked around him.

'All set?' he asked in hushed tones.

The rest nodded.

'Now! Grandpa!' Ronie signalled, by opening out a wing and closing it back, like a patriot thumping his chest.

They all held their breath. Grandpa uncorked his bottle of ale and left it on the floor, at the centre. And they all waited. And waited. Never was a wait so edgy, so tremendously heart thumping, and fraught with such killing uncertainty. Neither were minutes this long. Grandpa noticed limbs trembling and tongues nervously running over dry mouths.

There was only stillness, no smoke.

And then there was deep breathing in and heavy breathing out. But still no smoke.

Tension was mounting. And just at that volatile moment, Dunu heard Brum sniffing the ground right outside the log wall of the tool shed. He had sniffed his way to the source of the vibration, caused by the outpourings from Hazel's pocket.

'No! No! O no! Please!' Dunu said under her breath. 'O my God! Not now, no!' she silently pleaded, first to Brum and then to whoever might stop the large dog from creating a ruckus just outside, against the wall of the shed; just when they needed all the quiet in the valley not to scare Jerutu. More time passed. Jerutu hadn't yet started moving and Brum hadn't yet stopped sniffing.

In fact, when he was sure that Dunu and the rest of them were inside the shed, he started pawing the walls of the shed from outside and began to let out low, short growls which, every now and then, turned into a whimper. Then he fell silent. Dunu wasn't even done with feeling relieved for his silence when there was a shattering bark that tore through the silence and made everyone jump up with a start. In the process, all careful planning went awry. However, the good that happened out of this chaos was that Jerutu was startled out of the bottle of ale. And as providence would have it, the first nose it reached up to happened to belong to Hazel.

Poor Hazel's eyeballs rotated to a squint to look into a smoky face that appeared at a matchstick's length away from her eyes. She therefore took some time to realize that the face looked like hers. And when she did, she let out such a horrendous scream, borne upon such a mouthful of wind, that it both scared and blew poor Jerutu away. The dissolved Jerutu once again gathered itself and was now hanging from the ceiling next to the lantern, looking like it. In the melee, the oowii-oowiis completely forgot about their strategy of pretending to enter their chosen container for Jerutu so that the soul would follow them and swoosh into it ahead of everyone. So now the tiny low shed had one scared soul darting about and impersonating objects inside it, six mortals equally scared of the immortal and two open bottles of fluid. And just as most well-planned things fail to happen as planned, when Jerutu entered the bottle, it entered the wrong one. It re-entered the bottle of ale. Everyone in the shed saw the smoke drifting into the ale bottle. And remaining there.

'Get Brum to bark, Dunu, hurry!' Ronie was quick to think.

'Hey Brum!' Dunu called him. 'I'm in here, boy, comie-comie!'

That set Brum barking his lungs out as he scratched and thumped at the wooden walls of the tool shed. Brum's barking once again scared Jerutu as it did a moment ago but this time the others were more in charge of their reflexes. All previous strategy having gone kaput, the new plan was to, well, follow no plan. The oowii-oowiis sat down close together while Hazel knelt close to the bottle of milk. Grandpa stared at the bottle of ale. And when Brum resumed barking after a moment's pause to fill his lungs with air, inside the shed too there was another gust of air that suddenly came out of the bottle of ale. Jerutu! The moment all the air was out, Grandpa quickly replaced the cork tightly on the ale bottle so that Jerutu could not make another dive into it.

'Still, everyone!' Sunny whispered.

And everyone went still. Brum continued to scratch outside but his fierce bark slowly turned into a low whine. Jerutu whizzed about the shed for a while before stationing itself in line with the oowii-oowiis and Dunu.

'Still,' Sunny said again, 'Hazelnut…'

'Hrrumph!' Hazel voiced her annoyance.

Ignoring that, Sunny just continued, 'Ready, keep the cap of the milk bottle in hand.'

Hazel gave an indiscernible nod, like a schoolgirl compelled to obey a master she didn't like.

'Now!' Sunny signalled Ronie, Sandie, and Dunu.

So, the oowii-oowiis put up a claw, a paw and a limb towards the mouth of the milk bottle, pretending to try to get into it. Jerutu sat still, observing them. Then of a sudden, it whizzed up to Dunu. Dunu quickly forwarded a finger towards the mouth of the milk bottle. The moment she did so, Jerutu elongated itself and while one end of it was still squatting on the ground next to Dunu, the other end reached up to the mouth of the bottle of milk. Everyone held their breath. Suddenly there was another loud bark outside and, in an instant, the part of the smoke that so long was squatting stubbornly on the ground, sprang up and followed the front end of the smoke trail into the milk bottle.

'Hazel, quick!' Dunu reminded her.

Hazel swiftly capped the bottle of milk. Jerutu was at last safe inside the bottle and was ready to leave for the gompa.

'Phew!' Grandpa sighed. Immediately, more phews began to fly about the room. Hazel handed over the milk bottle to Grandpa. He held it carefully and close to himself before opening the door and letting everyone out. Grandpa followed the rest out of the shed and slowly walked away towards the house.

After all the excitement and confusion, only one thing remained to be done. Wait for Owl to return.

15

Into His Bollong

It was the darkest hour before dawn and Owl had already arrived at the swing post. Girim Umata saw him the moment he alighted because he had, without realizing it, been looking that way every now and then all through the night, anticipating Owl. But now that Owl was there, he was both eager and at the same time hesitant to go and meet Owl. Yet, he had to get over with this.

'Owl?' Girim Umata walked out to the swing. The cold wind shrieked past the mountain tops, gnawing through Grandpa's nightshirt and sweater. It sounded like an old, forgotten song of some mountain gnome. Grandpa, however, didn't hear anything of it. He heard instead the sound of lapping waves of merciless water swirling all around him, tearing him apart, devouring him bit by bit. And rising from those waters, he heard the woebegone voices of Pholey Deehang and Bawlungbwrai. One moment they were crying out piteously, pleading to be saved. The next moment they were laughing at him, their laughter hoarse and shrieking, making up the winds that howled through the mountains. And he walked through the retreating darkness to the swing to meet Owl.

'Southwest from here, by the Dwisikhlaa, lie miles and miles of nothingness, Grandpa,' Owl reported, 'but yes, there is the temple. No sidewalls, only damp, rickety posts painfully holding up a battered roof just above the stone shivling. No sign of abandoned huts, no sign of humans, no Fhuwanji. Only water. The river, Grandpa, she's everywhere.'

Owl did his best to describe to Grandpa a view of what he wished to see with his own eyes but had to settle for seeing through Owl's. As Owl narrated his trip, Grandpa regretted not being able to see his Fhuwanji once more. At the same time, somewhere deep inside him, he felt relieved that he wasn't there to see Fhuwanji in its watery tomb. He would not have been able to bear it.

An ache crawled into Girim Umata's heart.

'The joukhoorei?' he asked.

'It's there. The way you saw it when you left Fhuwanji.'

Guilt knocked at Girim Umata's conscience.

Would he have resurrected Fhuwanji? Was it actually meant to be Fhuwanji and not the emancipation of the Jerutus?

Turmoil surged in him once again, but Old Monk's words rang in his mind through that turmoil.

That which is destined to be, will yet be.

Girim Umata wouldn't go back on his decision about where to take Jerutu.

A cockerel crowed in the valley below and mellow rays of dawn brightened the eastern sky beyond the mountains. The wind ceased to scream. The sun's rays would gradually fill up the sky and usher in a new day, the Vesak Poya day. Thapa saddled Barhonka and Poohor and tied up the milk-can hanging from Barhonka's side. Dunu too had been up early. Hazel had hurriedly stuffed her with warm porridge and bundled her up well and fat with woollens.

'O dear! Is that me or an Eskimo!' Dunu exclaimed standing in front of the mirror.

'The higher reaches of Mount Swrang can be ruthlessly cold, child,' Hazel justified her act of dressing Dunu thus, 'and the wind! Oh! I shiver to even talk of it. It whips through every layer of clothing and bites into the bones, you see, now don't you take off any of those woollie-warmie-wobblies, mind you!'

As for herself, that day was one of those very rare occasions when Hazel had left her apron behind. She instead wore a pretty skirt that fell around her ankles, with a pristine white blouse; for she was going to the gompa with much devotion in her heart, which reflected in her dress. She covered her head with a soft pink, silk scarf which she had folded into a neat triangle, placed the longest side of the triangle just above her forehead and brought the two corners over the ears, before lightly tying them below her chin. She left the third corner lying on her back. That morning though, she covered her head not in fear of getting her hair into food. Today it was in reverence to her Buddha. Over everything, she had pulled on a fur coat of a happy, brilliant yellow. She looked like a walking sunray. Hand in hand, the two girls went out to the little group of pilgrims assembled and waiting by the kitchen.

Grandpa picked up Dunu and sat her astride Barhonka. Then he himself rode on Barhonka, behind Dunu. Thapa helped Hazel onto Poohor and then helped himself after her, on to whatever measly space remained on the horse's rear. Sandie helped herself onto Poohor's mane and Ronie perched on Grandpa's shoulder. Grandpa hung the bottle of milk on his left side, on a belt which he slung over his right shoulder and let it go all the way left across his big belly. Sunny hopped and skipped along and Owl was already way ahead.

It was a melange of precious beings, which embarked on an equally precious mission to the Dendup Gompa. It was also a melange of feelings that the beings carried in their hearts to the gompa. On one hand, there was a feeling of triumph at being able to find the Jerutu and take him to the bollong that waited for its soul on the Tree of Emancipation. On the other, there was also the sense of failing the joukhoorei, which too had waited just as did the bollong, for its soul. There was a sense of gratitude at being bestowed the opportunity to visit Dendup Gompa for Vesak Poya, but there was also a sense of grief, even in Hazel, to have to eventually say goodbye to Jerutu.

Having said not a word, having shared not a hug, the hundredth Jerutu had smoked its way into all of their hearts. They all wanted to protect it, to play with it. Now when it was time to send it off did realization dawn on them, how much they came to love it. Ache seeped into their hearts. 'Strange are the ways of Creation,' Grandpa made an effort to explain to the solemn group, 'it first attaches, only to gradually detach. Because, perhaps, the powers of the cosmos say that attachment is but illusion. Maya. And that detachment is the only truth. Although, I know not how.'

Now as Barhonka and Poohor clip-clopped up the mountain track, the group could understand neither Maya, nor the all-encompassing truth. They only understood sadness at having to part with Jerutu. It was a silent group that moved ahead. The track that day was not the one through forests and ravines, which the oowii-oowiis had taken on their earlier trip to the gompa. This one had a proper track, though narrow, which spiralled up the mountain like the ridges on a screw. And it seemed longer too.

Sandie, however, decided to lighten the moment and cleared her throat. And because tonight would be a full-moon night, she anyway would sing her noble heart out. As always, Ronie and Sunny would then join in. So, Sandie began to sing...

A- telling me, O Hazel! O Ronie!
A- telling me, O Dunu! O Sunny!
Why this goodbye be making us a-blue?
Why we a-sad to let go Jerutu?

Telling me before a-reach yonder gompa,
Before round moon a-rise on Vesak Poya,
Shouldn't all o' us be a-feeling glee,
For all ye Jerutus be flying free?

Ronie and Sunny sang in chorus...

He had no eyes to look into
A beautiful soul we yet saw through,
We felt scared, we felt happy
In each other's company!

But it was love above all
That did us all enthral
Though he sang no happy song
To all our joys did yet belong!

'S why, 's why, O! Sandie dear
To part and say goodbye we fear
'S why this goodbye's making us blue
'Coz we'd started loving Jerutu!'

Until now Grandpa had been bowing to passing monks and only listened to the song; he hadn't joined in. However, slowly, he too got drawn into the song of the oowii-oowiis. And soon, started singing along.

To love and to let go
Yet let in your hearts the fondness grow
That's the deepest mystery of Creation,
Loved and held close, even past separation.

Come every snow and every rain
Wherever you or I remain,
When smoke curls up from a winter fire
We'll know it's you, Jerutu dear.

When moon-dust rolls down upon the farm
All o' us, even big boy Brum,
Shall remember you again and again
Though you'd be gone to the mystic domain!

Be that why a goodbye is said,
To keep the heart from a-feeling sad?

> *Goodbye then, Jerutu, go whoosh free,*
> *In our hearts we'll cherish thee!*

And the oowii-oowiis once more fell into chorus…

> *In sorrow we shall not send you*
> *Go in glee with our love for you,*
> *In our hearts we'll cherish you*
> *JE—RU—TU…*

The sun was slowly sinking into the western horizon, behind the long rows of the high and low peaks in the Himalayas, when Girim Umata and his entourage arrived at the gates of Dendup Gompa. There were a few stone steps from the gate leading up and from there on, the rest of the yard was a beautiful, undulated, expanse. That day of course, little marquees lined the periphery, to house makeshift horse-sheds, cooking sheds with gigantic iron cauldrons, and resting area for the pilgrims. It was a moment of great wonder for all of them.

When they got off Barhonka and Poohor, they set foot on a ground that seemed to be at a wholly different sphere, a world where the mortal converged only to experience the eternal. The rise and fall of chants were punctuated by the booming resonance of gongs, and then led again by the blowing of long, decorated and curved horns. Dunu and Grandpa were left speechless with amazement. More so, because it was their first visit to the gompa. The bright red, blue, green, yellow and pristine white of the silk prayer flags playfully broke the monotonous maroon of the monks' robes. The enchantment of the Vesak Poya rituals was already gathering and gaining momentum. A villager came forward through the crowd to help Thapa lead Barhonka and Poohor towards the shed for horses. Before sending him off, Grandpa reminded Thapa to deposit the can of milk at the place of offerings for the sweetened rice.

Girim Umata held the bottle of milk close to him and Hazel didn't let go of Dunu's hand. They didn't know where or how to begin.

'We must look for Old Monk,' Ronie suggested.

'In this crowd?' Hazel wondered. Her command, she knew, would not run there. She could not send a scream flying, as she did back in the farm to summon Joyan and the rest of the boys. Just then, Owl flew down and landed on Grandpa's shoulder.

'Hey! Good to see you, fella!' Sunny squealed. 'Now guide us through, please!'

'Old Monk is at the feet of the Buddha,' Owl informed, 'inside the main altar, with the head monk of the gompa. He seems to be anticipating something. Or someone. Perhaps you. Or Jerutu. Walk into the prayer hall. There are people there, but not that you cannot walk through. Go, see him at once.'

They obeyed Owl.

❧

The smell of burning incense and yak-milk butter, the fragrance of fresh mountain blooms of spring, the chants in bass tone that seemed to rise from inside the head, everything caused a shiver to run beneath the skin. It all felt so dreamlike, so divine! The energy that rose from the continuous hum of mantras kept the minds of all who gathered there shielded from all elements with negative vibes and earthly distractions. And thereby opened their thoughts to the only truth of the universe, the final deliverance. Nirvana. Which Jerutu would attain that night. The prayer wheels and the prayer flags, each was serving its own purpose, unperturbed by the other. Yet, they served in harmony.

Hazel couldn't really understand what gave her the chills, the cold wind or this surreal ambience. Inside the gompa, she saw the grey, stone lamp, as if it were a football with its top cut open.

Dunu tugged at Hazel's coat sleeve. 'Look, Hazel!' she whispered, 'that lamp, it's different from the rest.'

Hazel bent to bring her mouth close to Dunu's ear. 'That lamp is as old as the gompa, child, and,' she whispered back, 'even older.'

Dunu's eyes sparkled, her mouth opened into a large 'O'. Every advancing step there stunned her more and more.

'That lamp,' Hazel went on, 'used to belong to a woodcutter named Karma Dendup, who lived hundreds of years ago, in this very place. The cottage in which he lived was rebuilt as this monastery.'

'Golly gimplink!' was all Dunu managed to say.

Old Monk saw them approach and he smiled. He gestured them to come forward, closer to him. 'Come, Girim Umata!' he said. 'I see you have the hundredth Jerutu with you. This is indeed an exalted moment! You have made great sacrifices.'

Girim Umata was yet to recover from the shock of being thus recognized by Old Monk, when the monk announced, 'Pholey Deehang is here as well.'

Girim Umata staggered back.

Old Monk smiled at the dishevelled, unshaven, wretched man next to him, shrunk from weariness of the body and the mind. From under his shirt and shawl jutted out his bony shoulders, the only reminder of firm, fine muscles that once wrapped those bones. He was reduced to a man who seemed to have given up on everything just as everything else had given up on him. He was by now disillusioned even with Bathou and with Baulungbwrai, to whom he had owed his highest devotion.

Not believing what he was just told, Girim Umata sat down in front of the man whom Old Monk introduced as Pholey Deehang and looked deep and long into his eyes. Yes, he remembered those eyes. They were the same eyes that shone during their childhood when they saw Girim Umata, but now they had lost their life. They were the same eyes that winked at Girim Umata to discreetly plan secret getaways during their adolescence. They were the same eyes that glistened with tears for Girim Umata when his wife had passed away. Yes, they were the same eyes, but the twinkle in them was gone. They were the same eyes, but now they stared back at Girim Umata, not recognizing him.

'Pholey Deehang?' Girim Umata called him, unsure of his own voice. 'It's me, Girim Umata.'

He reached out and placed a hand on Pholey Deehang's. Those same hands, but how scrawny they had turned! Lean, dark veins snaked beneath their coarse, papery skin, like the many streamlets that flowed down the rugged mountains. The face turned away for an instant, as if searching where the voice came from. When it again came to face Girim Umata, the eyes looked right through him into the crowd. Girim Umata's heart sank. Pholey Deehang was a silent symbol of

Fhuwanji in the ten years that had gone by. Girim Umata had lost him too.

'Pholey Deehang is here to take the lost soul of the joukhoorei back to the Bathou temple,' Old Monk said.

Girim Umata suddenly stood up and tightened his grip over the bottle of milk.

'Fear not, Girim Umata, Pholey Deehang has always been your friend and even at this hour of intense test, he has decided as you have. He has decided to let Jerutu attain emancipation. Girim Umata dropped on his knees and broke down. The lid that held back the turmoil of the past few days had come off and he held Pholey Deehang and sobbed his old heart out, resting his head on Pholey Deehang's skeletal knees. And along with the tears, he let go of all attachments with Fhuwanji, with old friends and roots, with his past. He sobbed them all out at the threshold of the Buddha, the compassionate, on Vesak Poya. Pholey Deehang, however, sat absolutely still, not understanding the reason behind this overwhelming outburst of grief, of a stranger, at his feet.

Much as they all had expected, there was no grand ceremony at the handing over of the bottle of milk with Jerutu in it to Old Monk. Girim Umata just held it out to him with both hands and Old Monk accepted with both hands, there at the feet of the Swrang Buddha, watched over by the Tree of Emancipation, and sung upon by all the monks around. That, though, in itself was an immaculate ceremony.

With dusk spreading over the mountains, the lanterns along the entrance of the gompa were lit up and innumerable lamps, some of ghee but most of yak-milk butter, drove away even the faintest shadow of darkness from the venerated grounds of the home of the Swrang Buddha. A chill breeze blowing from the north gently rotated the wind prayer wheels on the west and waters of the Dwisanchi danced past the water wheels in the east of the gompa, letting the prayers inscribed upon these wheels echo through all elements. And upon an earth thus bejewelled with sparkling lamps, perfumed with virgin flowers and incense and cleansed with prayers, the full moon of Vesak Poya rose into the vastness of the Himalayan sky.

Old Monk led Pholey Deehang, Girim Umata and Dunu, the oowii-oowiis, Owl and Hazel out of the prayer hall towards the Tree of Emancipation. Grandpa and Dunu were absolutely dazed at the magnificent sight of the Tree. Pilgrims had wrapped new, pristine *khatas* around the lower reaches of the trunk as offerings. In the light of the lamps, these made the tree look like it had a silver trunk. A haloed, comforting nebula of light rose above it, from the combined radiance of the bollongs and the jaikhlongs. The oowii-oowiis were equally spellbound. The same breeze that moved the wind prayer wheels now blew among the bollongs to make them sway gently on their golden yarns. Old Monk stepped onto the colourful reed mat that was spread under the Tree of Emancipation and sat down on it. He asked Pholey Deehang, Girim Umata and the rest of Jerutu's friends to come forward and sit close around him. A whole group of monks, priests, villagers and pilgrims, young and old, men and women gathered around them.

At last Old Monk spoke. 'Our final moment is not far now,' he said, with a calm that was in complete contrast to the unrest of those facing him. 'You have all served the purpose of your lives and have gained merit for your own emancipation, when the time for the same arrives.'

Dunu clasped Grandpa's hand.

'Pholey Deehang and Girim Umata have both given up interests of the self for greater good. When you both go back from here to live your lives, you will find triumph in the unexpected, and satisfaction thereupon.' Old Monk paused to look at Girim Umata. 'But when you go back, Girim Umata, you shall go without the Jataka creatures. So Bathou says. Because they have shown atonement of a past birth and have also served the purpose of the present one. Their time for emancipation has arrived.'

Dunu's heart suddenly felt hollow, and her stomach squirmed. She buried her face in Hazel's lap. Hazel held her close. When she looked up at the oowii-oowiis, she saw deep calm upon their faces, a calm that surpassed all panic and grief associated with parting. There was, on their faces, only intense bliss and love. For everything, for everyone.

'Especially for you, Dunu,' Sandie whispered, as if she read Dunu's mind.

The moon rose higher and higher into the Vesak Poya night sky. Old Monk stood up, closed his eyes and held the bottle of milk upright with his right hand, on his open left palm. Like a cup on a saucer. The bottle was still tightly closed. And then he started chanting prayers. Everyone around him stood up and joined their hands in prayer. There was an uncanny resemblance of the upright milk bottle on Old Monk's hands to the erect shivling on its oblong stone base at the Bathou temple at Fhuwanji. As Old Monk immersed deeper and deeper into his chants, outside in the waters of the Dwisanchi near the water prayer wheels, a vision appeared and dived in to appear again. A vision that appeared on full-moon nights.

Mertle.

The Vesak Poya moon's light shone down upon the shell on her back and bounced off to enter the tiny droplets of water she sprayed up with a splash of her elegant tail. And a sparkling mist of glodew rose. They poured in among the people, looking for Pholey Deehang.

Deep, resonating gongs and cymbals were now beating at intervals. Gradually, they began to boom more frequently. The combined passion of chants, hymns and *dungchens* began to swell, level by level, until it rose to an all-encompassing euphoria that reached past the mountains, up into the vast nothingness of space.

Old Monk slowly sat down again.

'I shall now open the lid of this bottle and the hundredth Jerutu will itself flow out of here, seek out its bollong and enter it. He will lay there for, and till, the final deliverance.' And he resumed chanting more prayers, before slowly removing the bottle cap as he said, thrice, 'Om Shanteihih! Om Shanteihih! Om Shanteihih!'

All sound and time seemed to have abruptly come to a pause. There were only lamps and their light. Everywhere. Silence was never so profound. A slow trail of smoke became visible inside the bottle of milk and soon, it started to curl out. It gradually rose towards the branches of the Tree of Emancipation. Tears welled up in Dunu's eyes and trickled down her cheeks as she watched Jerutu. Today, it didn't pretend to look like anyone. She kept looking without blinking. Jerutu sailed among the bollongs until it came to the one kept for him and without much of a goodbye, disappeared into it.

> *Go then, be free, Jerutu,*
> (Dunu heard the song in her mind)
> *Go in glee with our love for you,*
> *In our hearts forever we'll cherish you*
> *JE—RU—TU…*

The moment the hundredth Jerutu returned home to its bollong, it fell asleep in it, exhausted from the escapades of the recent past and lulled by the hum of all the prayers around. Dunu clung tight to Hazel and cried like she had never before. Her little self trembled all over. The harder she shook, the tighter she held Hazel, trying to stop the sound of her cries from being heard.

Old Monk was all along looking at Jerutu till he disappeared into his bollong on the Tree, but now he looked down from the Tree to Pholey Deehang and Girim Umata's little group and smiled. 'So now, before the divine moment of the emancipation of the hundred Jerutus arrives, do any of you seek to know anything about the great mysteries of the universe?' he asked them.

'Who are you?' Girim Umata asked, on an impulse.

'That does not pertain to the mysteries of the Universe,' Old Monk replied calmly.

'It does,' Girim Umata insisted.

'It does? How?' Old Monk asked.

'It does,' Girim Umata repeated, 'the universe comprises every being in it, however small or great. You are a being in the universe, Old Monk, and by that reason, you are part of the universe. Hence, I beseech to know about the part of the universe that comprises you. Who are you, Old Monk?'

'The Vesak Poya prayers have enlightened you, Girim Umata, come closer and sit by me,' Old Monk yielded.

Girim Umata held his breath as he came forward and sat near Old Monk.

'I am told,' Old Monk recollected, 'I was found in some village by the Dwisikhlaa, long, long ago, maybe about a decade. I lay bruised, unconscious and washed ashore by ravaging floods in the Dwisikhlaa downstream. Villagers around there noticed my bald head, the beads around my wrist and my mongoloid looks, which they related to a Tibetan monk's,' he smiled at that, 'and they took me for a Buddhist monk and brought me here. I have been here since.'

'Baulungbwrai!' Girim Umata exclaimed in disbelief.

He suddenly recollected what the oowii-oowiis had narrated to him upon their return from the gompa, words which Old Monk had told them. *'The soul is instinctively searching for, and is gravitating towards, the one thing or being with whom it shares a bond of long decades.'*

'The lost soul of the joukhoorei was searching for, and gravitating towards Baulungbwrai! Towards Old Monk!' Girim Umata thought, once more trying to fit together the remaining pieces of the puzzle.

If only he had, even for once, seen that face under the hooded robe at the Bathou temple in Fhuwanji all those years ago. If only.

'Baulungbwrai!' He found himself saying again.

Old Monk looked back calmly at Girim Umata. 'I am? But it's too late. Jerutu's gone. To his bollong.'

16

The Final Deliverance

Soon the Vesak Poya moon rose to the highest in its journey across the boundless skies over the mighty Himalayas and arrived over the Tree of Emancipation. Girim Umata, Pholey Deehang, Dunu, and Hazel looked up at it just as did every pilgrim and every monk, every teacher and every disciple from monasteries near and far. The moon too looked down upon all of them, as it did upon Fhuwanji, upon the Bathou temple and upon Dwisikhlaa from its place up there. It also saw the two palm trees, on the highest grounds of the Umata farm.

A captivating rhythm of gongs, conch shells, and fervent prayers rose and rose till it reached the moon. Every emotion that had been bound to the worldly too had lifted with that rhythm, allowing peace to descend. Peace, though not necessarily quiet. Because the hearts pounded loud. The hour had come. Old Monk raised his hands above his head and looked up at the Tree of Emancipation. It glowed brilliantly in a mist of moonshine, and the wind that whispered through its sacred branches seemed to sing Guru Rinpoche's hymn.

Hung Orgyen Yulgi Nubjang Tsam
Pema Gesar Dongpo La
Yatsen Chok Gi Ngodrup Nye
Pema Jungme Zhe Su Drak
Khor Du Khandro Mangpo Kor
Khye Kyi Jesu Dak Drup Kyi
Jingyi Lap Chir Shek Su Sol
Guru Pema Siddhi Hung

Hazel would later explain the hymn to Dunu…

In the northwest border of the Land of the Oddiyana
In the heart of a Lotus Flower
Endowed with the most marvellous attainments
You are renowned as Padmakara, the Lotus born
Surrounded by hosts of Dakinis
Following in your footsteps
I pray to you, come grant me your blessings!

And then the winds stopped. It stopped every other sound that was mingling in it. Silence fell upon the gompa like it would upon the loftiest mountains, in the stillest hour of night. Suddenly, cutting through that silence, Old Monk's gentle voice came.

'Repeat, my good folks,' he said to everyone there.

'Now. Om Mane Padme Hum!' He paused for the congregation to repeat.

'Om Mane Padme Hum…' it repeated after him.

'Om Mane Padme Hum!'

'Om Mane Padme Hum…'

'Om Mane Padme Hum!'

'Om Mane Padme Hum…'

'Om Shanteihih! Om Shanteihih! Om Shanteihih!' Old Monk finished the chant.

A light breeze moved out of the main prayer hall and wafted through the people. It gradually blew up to the Tree of Emancipation and a gentle glow appeared above the blessed tree, a glow that heightened the radiance of the nebula that was already shimmering there. And then the deliverance began! Soft hazes of light started to swirl out from the bollongs, moving heavenwards. The bollongs had at last liberated the Jerutus in them. The jaikhlongs too gradually started to dissolve, releasing a delicate spray of sparkles that swam out to merge with the luminous haze of the bollongs. All of them together formed an illuminated arch that rose and fell, almost as a floating roller coaster made only of light, which reached across the Vesak Poya night sky to blend with the eternal. Had they made any noise, they would have probably created the most soothing, melodious, tinkling ever, like minuscule crystals falling upon a stone floor. But they didn't. Like all activity in the cosmos, this very special journey of the liberated souls too was made in perfect silence and timing.

Old Monk stood mesmerized at this splendid sight of the final deliverance of the Jerutus, and of all other souls in the thousands of jaikhlongs on the Tree of Emancipation. His purpose in the Dendup Gompa had been served. Dunu failed to understand the whirlpool of emotions that tossed and shook her tiny being. There was awe at the magnificent experience; there was grief at having to part first with Jerutu and then with the oowii-oowiis; there was also gratitude at having someone still left for her to come back to, for having someone to give her a hug when she needed one—Grandpa and Hazel. But she couldn't stop her tears from flowing.

As the Jerutus floated out of their bollongs, they detached from the Tree of Emancipation and gently, one after the other, fell to the earth. One such bollong fell upon the ground and rolled away towards the waters of the Dwisanchi. It would have fallen into the waters there and crashed as the Dwisanchi swept it over rocky creeks and dashed it against crevices of the mountains, had Mertle not stopped it and held it aloft. She too had been watching the liberation of the souls from near the water prayer wheels, and had kept a track of the bollong where the hundredth Jerutu swam in. So she knew that it was the same bollong which rolled to her and was now in her care. She splashed up more droplets of water and there was another spray of glodew that wafted towards Pholey Deehang.

'Glodew!'

Pholey Deehang heard the familiar whisper and looked around. Sure enough, there was glodew. Upon his heart. Soon he heard the familiar voice in his head. That same voice, without any sound.

'Return to the Bathou temple before the moon wanes,' the voice told him, 'the bollong of the lost soul of the joukhoorei will be there.' Saying just so much, the glodew lifted and floated away, letting him once again hear that same whisper.

'Glodew!'

Pholey Deehang immediately and as quietly, jostled his way out through the crowd, which was still in a state of rapt enchantment at the sight of the magical phenomenon.

Everyone had their heads still turned skywards, and so no one saw Pholey Deehang walking away. Nor did Pholey Deehang wish to be seen leaving thus, because at that moment, he neither had the inclination nor the time to answer the whys and wherefores that would come his way if his exit was noticed. Even if he had the time or the inclination, he wouldn't know what explanation to give. So Pholey Deehang left the gompa and set out on his return journey. The prayers resumed, but their intensity was lesser now and the celestial arch was slowly narrowing and receding into the darkness of the night sky.

As Pholey Deehang moved out, only Old Monk saw him. The night was still up, though the liberation ritual was done. Some villagers were starting to move out of the gompa and return home. One such villager from the far south, further south of what was once Fhuwanji, offered Pholey Deehang a ride with him on his yak. Mertle leaped and bounded downstream along the waters of the Dwisanchi, carefully holding the bollong above the splashing waters with her fins. It could well be just the empty bollong, yet she carried it to Bathou with utmost zeal and devotion.

Mertle raced down the Dwisanchi with the bollong, looking up every now and then to see if the Vesak Poya full moon was still up. It was. She had to reach Bathou's home and the joukhoorei before the moon paled at the break of dawn. Many a time she hurt and bruised herself as the stream rushed over sharp edges and steep drops down craggy surfaces of mountain rocks. But she did not wait to soothe her wounds. She was racing against time. During one such severe collision on a jagged turn, the shell on her back came off. Excruciating pain sliced through her like a knife through a beetroot. She cried bitterly, but did not stop. She instead held her shell like a bowl in her raised fins, placed the bollong in it, and continued. Blood gushed out into the water as if it truly was a beetroot that had been sliced and washed.

The moon was yet bright but not at its brightest as it was an hour ago. Mertle hurried. She could still gain speed when she swam down the Dwisanchi along its currents but once the Dwisanchi fell into Dwisikhlaa, Mertle had to swim upstream, against the flow of the waters. She fought against her draining strength and flinched at the sharp pain that was now spreading all over her body. But she struggled through the agony and pushed upstream. She still hoped to make it to the joukhoorei before the Vesak Poya full moon was dulled by the rising sun at dawn.

Pholey Deehang was also approaching Fhuwanji. However, riding on yak back, he could not keep pace with Mertle. He too kept looking nervously at the moon. His fellow rider had introduced himself as Tagom, and his yak as Caspo. He initiated stray conversation to break the monotony of the journey, but Pholey Deehang could reply only in monosyllables. Because his mind was elsewhere.

'What thought may take the peace away from your mind, my good man, after this marvellous spiritual experience?' Tagom finally asked Pholey Deehang, unable to hold his curiosity about Pholey Deehang's absentmindedness.

'Ah, well, I have to get back some place before daybreak,' he replied.

'And why didn't you say so earlier! Come then, Caspo, faster, boy, faster!' he egged his yak on, 'and what place, my friend, do you need to reach before day breaks?'

'My temple,' Pholey Deehang replied.

'Of the Buddha?'

'Of Bathou....'

'Good then. Since I go that way, I may as well drop in to pay my obeisance,' Tagom said.

'But it's in ankle-deep water. In the middle of nowhere,' Pholey Deehang told him.

'But that nowhere is also somewhere, isn't it, my good man?' Tagom laughed at his own humour. 'When I have come this far, why not a little farther?'

And the men rode down the mountain towards what was once Fhuwanji. Tagom sometimes whistled a folk tune and sometimes tried to sing the words, though it was clear that he didn't know them by heart. Pholey Deehang found it amusing, though only momentarily. He knew that the bollong Mertle was so faithfully bearing down to the temple was empty. Yet, hope of the human mind could be amazingly compelling, and it had once again resurged in Pholey Deehang's mind. The men went on, towards Fhuwanji.

Meanwhile, Mertle had already arrived at Fhuwanji. She could see the Bathou temple, the stone shivling erect as ever, and the Joukhoorei slung across it. The moon was still up but it would not remain so for long. She looked around for Pholey Deehang, but he was nowhere around. He was yet to reach. She decided not to wait, for the moon would not. Suddenly she was gripped by a strange panic, of realization. 'Wouldn't the bollong be empty?' she shuddered. But she had gambled and taken pains. So now, there was no looking back.

She herself could not swim in shallow, ankle-deep water to reach up to the joukhoorei, so she set a-sail her upturned shell with the bollong in it. She then pushed as much water after the shell as she could with her fins and tail, making it float towards the shivling. The shell slowly floated away from her and just as it reached the shivling, it floated out again. Mertle was beginning to get disheartened. Strength and hope were abandoning her. Yet she splashed more water towards the shell. After going round and round for a while, the shell with the bollong finally reached the oblong base of the shivling. It got wedged upon a side and remained there.

Mertle was getting restless. The moon would soon start to wane, but Pholey Deehang had not yet arrived. She swam up and down the Dwisikhlaa near the Bathou temple to see if anyone was coming that way, if Pholey Deehang was approaching. After much restlessness and what seemed like an eternity, she saw three figures approaching on foot. Two humans and one animal. And because the animal refused to wade through the water, the men tied it to a tree and waded up to the temple. It was Pholey Deehang. And Tagom.

As Pholey Deehang hurried towards the shivling, he saw the bollong, floating on a strange vessel. It looked partly familiar, yet Pholey Deehang couldn't remember where or when he had seen it. Or if he had seen it at all. Yet, it looked familiar.

'This is my temple, Tagom, this is my Bathou,' he told Tagom, pride filling his heart.

'Now that I have come this far to the home of your God, my friend, I have to offer something at his altar.' Tagom searched on his person and pulled out a tiny, round, metal jar from the inner pocket of his robe. 'I have nothing other than this grape juice,' he said with apology but with reverence.

'Anything, Tagom, that comes with devotion in the heart,' Pholey Deehang smiled.

'So be it then, my friend, for you, your Bathou and your joukhoorei!' Tagom said, as he poured the grape juice on the shivling, a greater part of which washed the shivling before trickling down into the joukhoorei.

'Jai Bathou!' said Pholey Deehang.

'Jai Bathou!' repeated Tagom.

The movement of the men around Bathou's altar caused tiny ripples around the base of the shivling and these ripples stirred and dislodged Mertle's shell with the bollong in it.

The stir disturbed and awoke a certain soul slumbering in the bollong all this while.

For, just as the bollong could have as well been empty, it could have as well had the hundredth Jerutu in it too. So, it did. The lost soul of the joukhoorei was in fact still slumbering in the bollong. Compared with the undisturbed bliss of his abode in the joukhoorei at the Bathou temple of Fhuwanji, his sojourn at the Umata farm had been one of immeasurable unrest and trepidation. Hence, he was overtaken by such exhaustion that once he entered the bollong, he got lulled to sleep with the hum of prayers. He remained in deep slumber until that moment back at the Bathou temple. After enduring prolonged fatigue, the gift of sleep became so profound that waking—even for the ultimate liberation—proved difficult, especially for a young soul.

And so it was that the hundredth Jerutu failed to wake in time to join the others on their journey toward emancipation. Instead, it remained behind in its bollong. Yet, in a twist of fate, the hundredth Jerutu fulfilled its purpose by occupying the final bollong in time for the Vesak Poya Emancipation. This ensured that all one hundred Jerutus were symbolically united during that sacred moment of deliverance.

Now, just moments before Pholey Deehang, Mertle and Tagom heard a cockerel crow to herald dawn, they saw a lazy, swaggering movement of smoke rising out of the bollong and flowing into the joukhoorei, which had, just moments ago, been filled with grape juice. Fluid. Which, over time, expedited by its storage in a metal vessel, had fermented into beer. Jou.

The lost soul of the joukhoorei had returned!

❧

Back in the Gompa, it was time for the oowii-oowiis to leave. They sat long under the Tree of Emancipation while Old Monk now led a smaller group of monks through more prayers and more chants. For repentance. And for redemption.

As the oowii-oowiis absorbed the prayers, they experienced a great exaltation of mind and body. Gradually, realization dawned on them as to why, on their earlier visit to the gompa, they had this eerie feeling that they had known the Tree of Emancipation and that they had coexisted. Indeed so, they had known this tree in a past life, upon these very grounds. But back then, the Tree of Emancipation was not a tree but was Karma Dendup, the woodcutter, who had taken care of them. However, when it was their turn to take care of him, the oowii-oowiis had abandoned Karma Dendup. Now the Vesak Poya moon shone down on the oowii-oowiis through this very tree, to remind them of the pet dog, which remained faithful to Karma Dendup till his death.

Ronie, Sandie, and Sunny turned around and saw the dog still sitting and watching Karma Dendup in its incarnation of the Tree of Emancipation. Just that, the dog was no longer a dog. It was the Swrang Buddha, Buddha who dwelt on mount Swrang. The oowii-oowiis had already gone through atonement but they were brought upon this present state just to give them a glimpse into their past births in which their souls fell. And now the time had come for their souls to rise. Higher and higher, till they merged with the infinite nothingness of space, the ultimate truth, as Old Monk had said.

'The Vesak Poya moon,' he had said, 'would enlighten the ignorant. Like it did the Buddha, it would do tonight to the oowii-oowiis. Like it was, then, the Bodhi Tree, it would be tonight, the Tree of Emancipation.'

Dunu clung to Grandpa, not knowing why too many things were happening, all at the same time. Her heart felt strange. It wasn't aching. Rather, it felt like it wasn't there at all. When she breathed, the corners of her mouth drooped, and she felt a hard lump in her throat. She suddenly tore away from Grandpa and brought Ronie, Sunny and Sandie into her tiny embrace. It was then that she began to sob. She now felt her heart back in its place too. But how it ached! It wanted to burst with pain. She started crying. The oowii-oowiis didn't stop her. They let her get over her tears. Still crying, she let the oowii-oowiis go. She ran back to Grandpa and held tightly to him again. Ronie, Sunny and Sandie walked up to Hazel.

'Dear Hazelnut…' Sunny had merely started when Hazel broke into sniffles and sat down to hold the three in her ample embrace. 'Forgive my silliness, O darlings! Go now, be free.' Her voice choked. 'But if you ever plan an earthly sojourn, please, O please, make it the Umata farm and give me the opportunity…' and she released her embrace to cover her face and cry into her palms. Grandpa didn't have the courage to see them go. He was looking the other way.

'Ho! Grandpa!' Ronie shouted.

'Ho! Ho!' repeated Sunny.

'You be a-staying great and good, dear Grandpa, us be a-watching over Umata farm!'

Grandpa waved, still with his back towards them. They saw how he shook.

Sandie then gingerly climbed onto Sunny's tail and moving close with Ronie, partly touching ground but mostly above it, the oowii-oowiis together swam away with a speed that could only be explained as magical. They whizzed far away towards the peak of Mount Swrang. Their goodbye rang into Dunu's ears till they faded from view as a rooster, a spider and a squirrel, to become three bright speckles of light. The prayers were now gradually softening and the goodbye song of the oowii-oowiis rose above them.

> *It won't be hard to say goodbye*
> *It won't be hard if you try*
> *For every time you touch your heart*
> *You'll know we're not at all apart.*
> *Love isn't to hold back, but let go*
> *Love is to let the fondness grow*
> *Even when we're no more near,*
> *Memories always hold us dear.*
> *Goodbye, sweet Dunu*
> *Goodbye to you…*

Dunu kept looking at the speckles of light till each of them blinked away into a spear of the snow trident on the peak of Mount Swrang. Some say the oowii-oowiis merged with Bathou. Folks at Kindoree believe they merged with the

Swrang Buddha. At that very instance, the skies glowed just beyond the Swrang Peak, above the trident. A rooster crowed and Dunu's eyes widened.

'Ronie?' Grandpa turned back to look over his shoulder, to look for the rooster.

'No, Grandpa, your hola-holas are gone,' Dunu said through her tears.

'Oowii-oowiis!' This time Grandpa corrected her.

Dawn was breaking and it was time to return home. Girim Umata looked around for Pholey Deehang, but he was nowhere at the gompa. He then walked up to Old Monk.

'Baulungbwrai?' he called the monk.

'The purpose why I was brought here by destiny is served, Girim Umata, now I shall go into retreat,' Old Monk said as he walked towards the prayer hall.

Pilgrims, devotees, and villagers were now slowly returning to their worldly lives, away from the gompa. Some were still in a trance due to the night's events as they walked out in silence. Each carried back, even if a very small part, yet a part, of the Buddha's calm and compassion. Thapa brought in Barhonka and Poohor towards Grandpa, Hazel and Dunu. The thousands of butter lamps were still glowing, and they would be left thus glowing, until the next night was through. Girim Umata took one last look all around him before climbing onto Barhonka. Hazel lifted Dunu and sat her with Grandpa, this time facing him. Drained of body and mind and sad at heart, the little girl leaned against her grandfather's comforting bosom and let her heavy eyelids come together. She felt a warm trickle of tears finding its way out even through those shut lids. Thapa helped Hazel onto Poohor and led the horses out of Dendup Gompa, back along the mountain track to Umata farm. Every now and then, they saw Owl above them, flying along homewards. Home, to the Umata farm.

The track down Dendup Gompa was a quiet one for Girim Umata, Hazel, and Thapa. Dunu had fallen asleep on Grandpa's bosom and saw a beautiful dream. In the dream, she saw a pink spider with ten limbs, a white rooster with blue, yellow and green tail feathers, and a weather cock on his head, and a squirrel with a streak of orange running down its back from his head. They were dancing and singing by a fire near the only two coconut palms in the whole of the Dorai range.

> *Sprinkles of moonshine*
> *Tonight did create magic divine*
> *O mortal beings of the immortal Earth*
> *Look at the enchanted by birth!*
> *We are not a mys-te-ry*
> *We are no gnomes of fan-ta-sy*
> *We are but the chosen three…!*
> *The oowii-oowii buddies are we…*

Only, in this dream, Dunu and Brum were part of the bonfire.

Will It Happen Again?

Epilogue

Years and years later…

Technology at last staggered up to the remote, breathtakingly idyllic valley of Kindoree.

And there was inaugurated the first-ever cyber cafe in the whole of Dorai range. Dunu and Grandpa went to see the amazing invention and with the aid of the counsellor there, Dunu googled 'FHUWANJI'.

A fateful past…

And an unpredictable future…

Were simply presented

… in six words, on an otherwise blank page…

Old Pholey Deehang never wakes up!

In Gratitude

As said Old Monk,
'That which is destined to be, will yet be...'

And the Universe aligns people, time, situations and vibrations for such to happen. Thus, *The Lost Soul of the Joukhoorei* was destined to be, now. So the Universe aligned for my literary agent turned dear friend, Preeti Gill, and editor-in-chief at Om Books International, Shantanu Ray Chaudhuri, to step in at this point in time and make the book happen. I am indebted to Preeti and Shantanu.

Despite being low on the health graph, Shantanu plodded through the manuscript, to edit it himself. The kind of enthusiasm with which he took to the planning of the book, getting the cover design done by Pinaki De, and getting involved with the script, was so encouraging! Perhaps I wouldn't work as hard myself. Thank you, Shantanu, though that isn't enough to really express all that I feel.

This book is as much Shantanu's, as it is mine.

I am overwhelmed with gratitude to the legend and maestro, Gulzar Saab, for taking time out not merely to read the story, but very generously, to write a few words for this book. I feel absolutely humbled and honoured to receive such words of profound encouragement from him. I am indebted beyond words, Bade Baba, thank you.

I am thankful to Pinaki De for the beautiful, catchy, cover.

This story is one of the closest to my heart, and one which I had begun narrating many, many years ago but for reasons deeply emotional and personal, had remained with me, unpublished. The narration began when our son Jerry was a mere toddler, and our daughter Sandie, my niece and nephews, Dunu (Sonali), Sunny (Vishal) and Ronie were very young. It is from them, and many more nieces and nephews, and pets, that I borrow the names of the magical, fantastical characters, of the rivers, the mountains and the hamlets, that make the story of the lost soul come alive. To them all, my love and gratitude, across all realms.

Casper, Doby, Eddie, Fido and Harley have let me hug them when I ran into my blues; and when I ran into a pen dead-end, they let me run with them and fetch a ball, have me pull a sock out of their mouths and taught me patience as they went about their outdoors business, till my pen resumed to flow. How can I ever thank my pet-babies enough who give such unconditionally? Yet I thank them, with oodles of cuddles.

Jayanta Das, Ranuj Mili, Hemen Rabha, Nirmik Marak and Bikhau Marak have been an amazing home-support system, without whom I would not have been able to do the amount of daydreaming, idling and imagining that I indulged in, of being in the village of Fhuwanji, pampered with cups and cups of tea and thin arrowroot biscuits. They may not even know that I have mentioned them here. But that does not matter. What matters is that I hold in my heart gratitude towards them, for the support they have lent, and still do.

I thank all my friends who unfailingly kept sending good wishes all along.

And to a very special, small and closed group of friends (you know who you are), I need you to please continue to walk with me. Thanks, and hugs!

My husband Hemanta doesn't read much! He may not read this far into the thanksgiving either. And yet, he would pop in at the oddest moment, while I write, asking if I needed a glass of warm water or a cup of tea! Thank you, Henry, that was much craved for.

Sandie, our daughter, had always been my unofficial and first reader, my best critic. Only, she sometimes got so involved in the story that she forgot to go into healthy criticism! Thanks, San, for all the times we read and discussed together.

I thank Jerry, our son, for his antics, gestures and inspirations, provided with the least of the spoken words. He is a child of action.

A huge gratitude goes to my extended family, friends, and my growing circle of fans, who have not yet disowned me for the kind of stories I tell. Which makes me believe that I may tell some more.

I am grateful to Providence.